WHEN T

WHEN THE RIVER SLEEPS

EASTERINE KIRE

ZUBAAN
128 B Shahpur Jat, 1st floor
NEW DELHI 110 049
Email: contact@zubaanbooks.com
Website: www.zubaanbooks.com

First published by Zubaan Publishers Pvt. Ltd 2014
Reprinted 2015

10 9 8 7 6 5 4 3 2

ISBN 978 93 83074 89 1

Zubaan is an independent feminist publishing house based in New Delhi
with a strong academic and general list. It was set up as an imprint of
India's first feminist publishing house, Kali for Women, and carries
forward Kali's tradition of publishing world quality books to high
editorial and production standards. *Zubaan* means tongue, voice,
language, speech in Hindustani. Zubaan publishes in the areas of the
humanities, social sciences, as well as in fiction, general non-fiction, and
books for children and young adults under its Young Zubaan imprint.

Typeset in Andrade Pro 11/15.9 by Jojy Philip, New Delhi 110 015
Printed and bound at Raj Press, R-3 Inderpuri, New Delhi 110 012

For JJ
and
his hunter son

ONE

Waking Dreams

VILIE PLUNGED HIS HAND into the river. It was cold – close to freezing – and perfectly still. It was just the way it should be. The river had gone to sleep. Everything was as the seer had told him. Almost imperceptibly, he slid forward and entered the water and plucked a smooth stone from the bottom of the river. In a similar motion, he pulled his arm out of the water and stood still. But it was too late. He felt through the soles of his feet that a great force had awakened. Before he could reach the shore, the water had swelled above his waist – the river had come alive! In an instant, the great torrents had tethered his legs in its twisting undercurrents, dragging him down forcibly into its depths. Vilie's struggles were feeble against the force of rushing water. Unable to reach the surface, his lungs began to burn for air and his mouth filled with water. He tried to shout, even as he felt himself being swallowed further into the darkness. Above his struggling form the river roared, drowning out his muffled screams. Then, in a final panicked outburst, he struck out against the power that was consuming him. His movements grew more frantic. A deep guttural sound escaped his throat. He flung out his hand and it hit the edge of the bed. It then dawned on him that he had been dreaming again.

Sweat drenched his face and neck. He threw off the covers and lay back trying to catch his breath. He had had the same dream every month for the past two years, ever since he had first heard the story of the sleeping river. He was restless in a way that he had never been before. And it made him come to a decision. The following week he would go on the wretched journey and get the river out of his head. But he didn't really mean it like that. Vilie was fascinated by the tale of the sleeping river. It was more than a story to him. He wanted more than anything to find the mysterious river, and 'catch it' when it went to sleep. Nothing else mattered to him. At least that was how he felt these days. It had become an obsession. He had told and retold the story to different bands of hunters who had come to him in the forest where he lived. Some of them shook their heads in disbelief. Others–like the young boy Rokolhoulie – listened in astonishment, absorbing every detail of Vilie's tale.

"Anie* Vilie, what do you mean by 'catching it' when it is sleeping?" Roko once asked.

---

* Anie: paternal uncle. Tenyimia usually address older men by this term.

Carefully choosing each word, Vilie responded:

"When the river is asleep, it is completely still. Yet the enchantment of those minutes or hours when it sleeps is so powerful, that it turns the stones in the middle of the river bed into a charm. If you can wrest a stone from the heart of the sleeping river and take it home, it will grant you whatever it is empowered to grant you. It could be cattle, women, prowess in war, or success in the hunt. That is what is meant by catching the river when it is asleep. That way you can make its magic yours. The retrieved stone is a powerful charm called a heart-stone."

"Anie Vilie, do you want to find the sleeping river?" asked Roko.

"Every hunter wants to find it, son. Will you come with me and look for it?"

"Oh yes, when I am big enough."

Vilie lay in bed, recollecting his brief exchange with the impressionable boy. Roko accompanied his uncle as often as he could to Vilie's shed in the forest. It was more than a shed now because Vilie had constructed an additional room so that if two groups of hunters should come at the same time, the second group need not be turned away. The forest was home to Vilie.

He had spent twenty-five of his forty-eight years here. He had no thought of returning to the village now, though his mother had time and again asked if he planned to have children, so she would have someone to take care of her in her old age. He had stayed on even after she died, and their

ancestral house began to fall apart. The clan then made him
guardian of the *gwi*,* the great mithuns that walked these
regions and fed on the tender young leaves of the *ketsaga*.†
The Forest department asked if he would like to become
the official protector of the rare tragopan that liked to nest
in Vilie's part of the forest. He agreed to this as well, and
they paid him a small salary in addition to monthly rations
of rice and salt, tea and sugar. Sometimes they would add
a bottle of rum.

Vilie was content with the way things were. He didn't
feel the need to marry. His aunts seemed to be giving up on
that project. After all, the forest was no place for a woman
and children. It was not important to him that he had no
heir to carry his name forward when he died. This had been
the argument his aunts pressed on him the most. However,
he had made up his mind, and his long years away seemed
to prove as much. As time went by, even his persistent
aunts accepted that he might never marry.

There had been a girl once, a very long time ago. It was
the gentle-mannered and tender-faced Mechüseno, for
whom the boys would climb the tallest trees in the woods
and pluck flowers. For some weeks Vilie had been certain
Seno cared for him too, and he wondered how he might
finally approach her. Many in the village expected they

---

* gwi – mithuns (bos frontalis) found in the hills west of Kohima. Some
are domesticated and reared by villagers.

† ketsaga – belongs to the tree fern family, an edible fern which is the
main food for the gwi.

would eventually find each other. However, a peculiar set of circumstances would soon put an end to such dreams.

It was the summer he turned eighteen, and the heavy monsoon rains had finally given way to warmer days. The late summer sun dried the muddy field-paths, and teased out the dragonflies. Everyone was out and about, preparing for the harvest season. Seno too went to the forest to gather herbs with two close friends. They climbed a tree to pluck a beautiful orchid that grew in its branches. When the three girls were making their way home, Seno said to her friends that a tall, dark man had climbed down the tree and was following them home. She kept looking back in fear. Her companions saw nothing at all. At the village gate they parted; Seno went home to her parents and was racked by a terrible fever in the evening. The fever would not leave her and on the third day she told those tending to her that the man from the tree was sitting by her bed.

"Send him away Mother, he is staring at me!" she cried out.

Her mother and sisters saw no one. She grew silent for many hours, and then suddenly let out a loud shriek, calling out over and over again: "He's got hold of me, Mother!"

Her face contorted in pain, and she threw her head back and went limp. Her mother and sister screamed in horror and tried everything they could to revive her, but she was gone. Seno was buried outside the village gate because she had died in what were considered 'ominous circumstances'.

Any clan member dying after encountering a spirit could not be buried within the village. Her family members were inconsolable, weeping for many days over the mound of earth that was her grave. Slowly and painfully they forced themselves back into working in the fields.

For many months, they noticed that someone had been leaving flowers at the lonely little grave. This went on for several months but suddenly stopped after Vilie began to make the forest hideout his home. His absence was felt in the community, and many believed that he had also passed to the other side. Rumours circulated that the two lovers used to meet in their spirit forms in the woods. As the years passed, the rumours slowly disappeared, and the events surrounding Seno's peculiar death, and Vilie's departure were soon relegated to village mythology, and only occasionally retold by Vilie's mates.

TWO

The Forest

"THE FOREST IS MY WIFE," Vilie had forcefully stated to them time and time again. Yet, his aunts continued to nag him relentlessly on the subject of marriage. He had said it only once to his mother, but his tone so shook her that she would never raise the issue again. In a way she understood her son despite her own longing for grandchildren. His aunts, however, persisted long after his mother had given up. The idea of a man living his life out in the forest – away from the communal life of the village – was so alien to them. The village was the only life they knew, and Vilie had stopped trying to explain why he preferred living on his own. It often made no sense to him either. He still went through months when nothing could touch him except that great loneliness that howled through his being like the wind baying up the valley, relentlessly beating at the wooden house and rudely blasting in through cracks in the walls. The sense of isolation was almost enough to make him abandon his life in the forest and return to the village.

In the second year, he felt so lonely he stopped all construction work on the shed. He still remembered the day he had been making a stone wall. He built it on the western side of the shed to shield it from the strong winds. It was then that the bleakness of the life he had chosen hit him. The feeling did not pass as it used to in the first months. It stayed like a persistent fever and settled into his bones. Though it was still light, Vilie gathered up his tools, placed them on the shelf and walked away from his house. What was this choice he had made? Was this really what he wanted for the rest of his life? Thoughts came to him of the village and what people would be doing in the late afternoons. Those in the fields would still be working under the open skies, perhaps chanting work-songs in a' call-and-response' way so typical of his people, to add rhythm to their toilsome labour. Life in the village would perk up as the old and the very young prepared to welcome back the singing field-goers. Vilie could picture them – the old women prodding at their hearths to get their fires burning for the evening meal. The melodious workers would be heard approaching from afar, homeward bound to warm evening meals and a well earned rest.

"It is those things that I miss," he thought to himself.

Not so much the festivals and feastings and the community gatherings, but the ordinary things of village life: the children fetching water in their small water-pitchers; the neighbours calling out to each other; and the village animals being shooed from the paths before they soiled them.

"Who or what would stop me if I should walk back to that life? Nothing and no one! I'm not answerable to anyone. The Forest Department can easily find someone else to come out and camp here at intervals and keep track of the tragopans."

The village council too had earlier coped without his help in looking after the *gwi*. He was not indispensable. But the question remained: what was stopping him from going back to the village? This question nagged him into the next day and prevented him from finishing the work on the stone wall.

"The forest is my wife."

He had said this many times to his relatives back at the village. Now he had the sensation that he was being an unfaithful spouse. He began to think that leaving the forest would be the same as abandoning his wife. Though it was an unsettling thought in his soul, he found he had actually nurtured it for a long time.

The following morning as the twinges of the all too familiar feeling of loneliness crept in, his own words returned to him.

"The forest is my wife, and perhaps this is what marriage is like; with periods when a chasm of loneliness separates the partners leaving each one alone with their own thoughts, groping for answers," he thought.

Strangely, these thoughts calmed him. He felt clearer in his head. He had strived so hard after something that was still elusive. Perhaps the answer lay not in striving but in being. In simply accepting that the loneliness would never be eliminated fully, but that one could deal with it by learning to treat it like a companion and no longer an adversary. It had been many years now since he had thought of the girl he had loved, Seno. Some days he could not remember her face. It became a blur to him and he had stopped trying to put features to the blur. So it was not a hankering after her that brought on this loneliness. It was just a part of being human.

The previous night's dream had momentarily brought back the same feeling of despairing emptiness. But he fought it hard, and this time it made him get up and collect the items that he would need for a long journey. He had an old canvas travel bag that one of the hunters had given him. The fabric was sturdy enough, so he flung it on his bed and began to fill it. He sheathed his hunting knife and tucked it into the bag. The knife was followed by a roll of tobacco and tobacco leaves in a pouch. He then packed a small packet of salt, a pouch of tea, some rice and dried beef and venison. He fetched a box of bullets that was half-empty, and added a handful of pellets and buck shot as well as six slugs. He added the two slugs on the table for good measure.

Vilie sat down momentarily and scanned the dark interior to see what else might be handy on a long trip.

He noticed a long rope hanging by the side of the window. He reached for the rope, coiled it and threw it into the bag with the other things. He topped off the bag with a rough woollen blanket, then closed it and tied it up with a leather cord and set it aside. He would need a day or two to put the shed in order before he could set out. He would plan an obligatory detour to the Nepali wood-cutters who were his only neighbours. Their settlement was four hours walk from his shed. From time to time, the woodcutters brought him sugar and tea from their trips into town.

His sudden impulse to pack had a significant effect on him. As he finally lay to rest that evening, he felt as if an enormous weight had just rolled off his back. He felt light-headed imagining his departure. It occurred to him that perhaps something had changed. Perhaps now he would stop dreaming about the sleeping river. As his eyes closed, his thoughts dwelt for a time on the question of the sleeping river.

"Is it possible that only forest dwellers can understand such things exist in the places not frequented by man? Will the magic of the river work only for a believer? Would it work in spite of lack of faith?"

The next day he mended the hole in the wire fencing around the house. The fence was intended to keep pesky animals away from his food rations. He reinforced it with medium sized posts. It was in fact high enough to deter larger animals. Then he turned his attention to the porch, where some planks had rotted in places. To prevent it collapsing, he pulled out planks from a pile of quarter-sawn pine boards he had purchased from the Nepalis. Vilie sawed them into four-by-four inch planks to match the existing ones. He then cut away and replaced the rotted planks. The work took most of the day, and it was dusk before he could prepare his evening meal. Nevertheless, it was gratifying to have finally finished work on the house that he had postponed all summer.

THREE

Neighbours

IT TOOK HIM FOUR-AND-A-HALF HOURS to get to the Nepali settlement. One of his traps had sprung and he found a big civet cat growling in the hole it had fallen into. One swift stroke of his knife and the cat was still. Vilie cut a strong bamboo pole and strung the cat on the end of it. He was sure the Nepalis would welcome the addition to their diet. Though the villagers called it a settlement it really was just a few sheds put together where the wood cutters had their colony. The men worked in the forest, cutting trees which they sectioned and sawed into planks. Three or four families lived there on a regular basis, but if the men found work they moved with their families to the other camps.

There were only two adults when he arrived, the woodcutter Krishna and his wife. The woman was suckling their infant son so the man prepared tea for Vilie, and gratefully accepted his gift, which he proceeded to skin and cut into small portions for cooking. The Nepalis had adapted to the forest diet of trapped wild animals. They liked to add chilli and spices to make a nice curry out of the wild meat.

"Krishna, I am going on a long trip. Would you look after the tragopans and report to the Forest Department if you see any hunters shooting or trapping them?"

Krishna looked up in surprise.

"Saab, you have never asked me that." Krishna always addressed him as saab.

"Well I have never been on a long trip before, so there was no need to ask you until now."

"How long do you think you will be away, Saab?"

"Three or four weeks, or two months, I'm not sure," Vilie answered.

He didn't want to admit that he was not sure if he would find what he was searching for. The whole trip was tinged with uncertainty. Yet, when he thought of his dream, he had no doubt he was meant to find the river. If he needed a sign, there could not be one clearer than that. Who knows what would happen after that? But he was not worried about the next step. He felt that he would know what to do when the time came.

A small squeal stopped his train of thought. It was the baby.

"How old is he now?" Vilie asked.

"Nearly four months, Saab. He is getting teeth already."

"What? Four months and getting teeth! That's quite early. Can I hold him?"

The mother came forward and handed the baby to

Vilie. There was no protest from the child. In fact, he was gurgling and happy to be held. Vilie did not remove the flannel cloth in which the child was wrapped. He wouldn't risk scratching the baby's tender skin with his calloused hands. He held the baby up in the air and drew him back to dandle him. The baby loved it.

"What are you going to do when he is old enough to go to school?"

"Saab, what do you mean? I am not a rich man. I don't have the means to send him to school. I will teach him my trade and he will grow up and earn an honest living. School is not for the likes of us, Saab."

Vilie paused and looked into the laughing face of the baby. Krishna was probably right. What could school possibly teach him that his parents could not improve upon? They were rich in their knowledge of the ways of the forest, the herbs one could use for food, the animals and birds one could trap and the bitter herbs to counteract the sting of a poisonous snake.

"I guess he will go to the best school then," Vilie remarked.

"You will be one of his teachers, Saab," Krishna said with a smile.

"That is a big job, surely the biggest I will have in my life."

Vilie's bag lay just inside the door to the wooden shelter which the Nepalis called home. Krishna looked over at it and Vilie followed his eyes.

"Saab, are you going to set off from here without returning home?"

"Looks like it, doesn't it?" Vilie responded.

Vilie thought about that. There was no good reason for him to postpone his journey any longer. In the bag was all he needed for the journey. He even had his gun with him. He didn't have a map but hunters in these parts did not use maps. They had mapped out the land in their heads. In fact, when an Australian researcher wanted to make a map of the Zuzie region, he used the hunters and their knowledge of places and place-names to construct a fairly accurate map.

"It's too late to travel this afternoon. Saab. Why don't you spend the night here and set off early in the morning?" Krishna offered.

Vilie looked at the sun in the horizon. It was probably two o'clock in the afternoon. He saw that the leaves on the plantain were already holding little pearls of moisture condensed from the heat. If he set out now, it would be dark before he could find a good place to spend the night. However, if he stayed at the Nepali settlement, he would get a head start the next day. Vilie planned to go in the direction opposite of Zuzie. By doing that, he would cross the first Zeliang villages before heading deeper into the forest.

"Thanks Krishna. I will do that," he said decisively.

"Good. I will cook the meat you brought and we can sleep early."

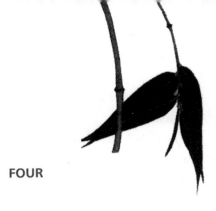

FOUR

Nocturnal Visitors

THE FLAVOUR OF THE MEAT WAS INTENSE, both from the spices Krishna had used and the gamey taste of the civit. The three of them were soon ready for bed. The meal had been heavy. Krishna laid two rugs over a wooden cot, and he gave Vilie an old blanket to use, apologising they did not have more blankets for the hunter. Vilie insisted that he was not accustomed to such luxury. Before he slept, he made sure Krishna had not given him blankets that they would themselves need.

When they put out the kerosene lamp, the sounds of the forest were the only noises they could hear for a long time. Owls hooting, frog calls and a host of insect sounds. Vilie turned over and fell fast asleep. He must have been sleeping for a good two hours when he was woken by a long drawn out yowl. It made his hair stand. It was a blood-curdling sound and seemed very close to the shelter. As he lay debating whether to get up and investigate it or ignore it as one of the many mysterious sounds of the forest, it came again, this time in a chorus of voices.

"Jackals!" Krishna swore loud enough for him to hear.

Vilie grabbed the gun from below his cot and sprang up. Krishna was trying to shoo them off with a big flaming firebrand. There were several of them, a whole pack, the big ones growling, unafraid of Krishna. The bigger jackals barked at the younger ones who were moving off at the sight of the firebrand. Vilie swung his gun round and aimed at the leader of the pack. He was in his prime. Bigger than all the rest, he flung himself at Vilie when he saw the gun. Vilie did not expect the charge and shot immediately, blasting a hole in its head so that it fell down flat on the ground, but not before Vilie had caught sight of the foaming mouth and the reddened eyes. After the leader fell, the rest dispersed rapidly, yelping as Krishna threw stones after them and found targets.

"Rabies!" exclaimed Vilie. "No wonder they came so close to the shelter and did not retreat at your fire scare!"

"They come for the chickens. Not only that, they know that there is a helpless human baby that could be food for them if their food sources run out," Krishna stated.

"That's dangerous! Have you got a gun? You mustn't take risks living like this in the jungle with a woman and a child!"

"Where would I get a gun from, Saab? I keep a pile of stones and my khukri sharpened and ready. So far, nothing has happened beyond a few disturbed nights and a couple of missing chickens."

"That's not right. You need a gun. I will insist on one for you and if your employer can't give you one, I'll sell my house and get you one."

"No no! You mustn't do that Saab! We are forest people. Our people have always lived like this. We will be all right."

The two of them dragged the dead jackal away from the shelter and dug a hole in the darkness, choosing to bury it right away rather than risk any animal feeding upon it. The clinking of the spade against loose stones was the only sound heard in the forest for some time. The jackals did not return that night.

Vilie lay down again. He could hear the jackals howling faintly in the distance. His trained ears could tell they were quite far off, perhaps headed in the direction of the Zeliang villages or other human habitation. When he woke again, the chickens were fighting over their grain. He quickly got out of bed, folded away his bedclothes, and ran out to splash cold water on his face. Krishna's wife poured him tea from the kettle. He scalded his tongue, and cursed under his breath.

"I overslept," he muttered.

He took a clean mug to cool the tea by pouring it from one mug to the other. They offered him some of the leftover food. He wasn't hungry but he forced some food down, knowing he would need it for the journey ahead. He was keenly aware that it could be hours before he found some source of food again. When he finished eating, he stood up and rolled a smoke and lit it. While Krishna stood watching, Vilie picked up his bag and lifted his hand in mock salute.

"Travel carefully Saab, the forest is dangerous to those who don't know it, but it can be kind to those who befriend it."

"I will be careful Krishna, and you two take great care of that precious treasure of yours. I promise you I will get you a gun on my return."

He walked out of the clearing and was soon swallowed up by the trees and plantain leaves.

FIVE

Weretiger

ALL DAY HE WALKED until he found a tree with branches close together. He climbed up and made a bed across three branches that looked as though they had served that purpose before. It was not the most comfortable place to rest, but he would be safe from snakes and bears and any other troublesome creatures roaming the forest floor. He slept soundly, woke before dawn and began to walk along a narrow path without stopping to cook food.

"If I cover a good distance, I can stop in the evening and find shelter before dark," he thought to himself.

When Vilie finally relented, the sun was close to setting. But he had made good time and was fairly close to a shed in fields belonging to a Zeliang man by the name of Keyireusap. It would be wise to camp there even though it was a few more hours to nightfall. To be caught out in the woods after dark without any shelter was to invite trouble.

In an hour, he was at the shed. He found heaps of straw to sleep on, a rough hearth and two pans to cook in. It was customary that the owner keep a couple of old pans, so that anyone who came to shelter in the shed could make use of them. He gathered firewood to supplement the stack that was already there. Two matchboxes were within easy reach. He shook the bamboo salt container and found that it was half full. The container was carefully covered with leaves to keep the salt from turning hard.

Vilie soon had a fire going. Dry leaves and twigs hissed and crackled as the fire steadily grew. He had carried rice in his bag so he put some handfuls into a pan, and added some of the dry meat. Filling the pot halfway with water, he placed it carefully atop the fire. A bit of salt went into the pot. Vilie went out to forage in the patch behind the shed to see if he could find some ginger. Sure enough there was a patch of country ginger growing, and he plucked some of the leaves for his pot.

It was good food. Dried meat and ginger leaves didn't need much additional seasoning. The ginger leaves were strong and pungent and complemented the meat. Vilie had even found some dried chilli in a bottle by the hearth which he used sparingly. The fire crackled and blazed fiercely as he stoked it. When the meat was tender, he took the pot off the fire and waited for it to cool. The sun began to set before he had finished eating. Afterwards, he covered the leftover food and set it aside. It would make a good meal for the next day and save him time on the road. He filled his mug with boiled water and drank it slowly. Finally he reached for his tobacco pouch and rolled himself a smoke, making a mental note to get a bundle of tobacco leaves on his way back. Lighting the home-made cigarette, he took a deep drag, and let the smoke curl its way upwards to the roof.

The pile of straw made a good bed when he covered it with an old rug he had found hanging on the door of the shed. He threw the coarse blanket over himself and lay back slowly. Get up before dawn and set off before sunrise, that was his plan.

"There is nothing quite like setting out early on a trip," he muttered to himself.

Vilie fell asleep almost immediately. At first he slept heavily – the sleep of the fatigued. But Vilie was a hunter and the slightest of sounds could wake him no matter how deep in slumber he was. It came as the softest fall of padded feet. Vilie woke with a start, the hair on his arms standing on end at the knowledge that he was not alone. He carefully reached for his gun and braced himself for more sounds. What could it be? A bear? His trained ears knew it was a bigger animal than the usual squirrel or porcupine. In fact, he was quite certain it was a very much bigger animal. Vilie sat upright in bed and waited tensely. He did not have to wait long. The intruder swung a paw at the wall of the shed and the night was shattered by the vile noise. A clattering followed the smashing of a great paw into old tin and weak wood.

Vilie shouted and cocked his gun instantly. He ran to the door of the shed and peered into the darkness trying to catch a glimpse of his assailant. The light from the fire was so dim he could only just barely make out the dark shape lunging toward him. The tiger came at him fearlessly, throwing itself at the outline of the man. At the last second, Vilie sidestepped and the tiger crashed into the door, breaking it, and leaving torn fragments of wood hanging on the hinges. Vilie shot off a bullet above the animal's head. The sound was thunderous and the tiger sprung to its feet and leapt away into the night. The blinding flash from the shot lit up the darkness momentarily, and he saw that the tiger was much bigger than any he had ever seen. Its back was almost as wide as the door it had smashed.

He had not wanted to kill the tiger if he could help it, and was pleased that the shot had had the right effect. He stoked the embers with fresh wood until he had a good fire going. Then he laid logs atop the fire so it would burn long into the night.

Vilie was not sure if the animal would return. At the same time he didn't feel he should go back to sleep. So he lay awake with his gun across his chest, cocked and ready. He had his finger on the trigger but the hours passed without him hearing anything. So he laid the gun by the bed, and with the fire going strong he dozed off.

SIX

Speaking to the tiger

VILIE DIDN'T SLEEP LONG. The tiger returned, this time roaring loudly as though it were in pain. Vilie woke and pulled his gun to him. Should he shoot and finish it off? He was quite used to shooting smaller animals for food but he had never shot a tiger. For one, he could not use it for food. Secondly, he would be obligated to perform the tiger-killer ritual which was complicated and not meant for a solitary hunter to fulfil alone in the forest. It was a ritual that required the presence of many members of the clan.

There was yet another factor which now came to mind when he heard the tiger returning. This could very well be a weretiger, Vilie thought. As a rule, ordinary tigers kept their distance from man. This one had been scared off by a gunshot and yet he was coming back for more. Vilie was quite sure by now that it was a weretiger. The folk practice of certain men transforming their spirits into tigers was a closely guarded art. Despite the secrecy, most of the villagers knew who were the men who had become weretigers. He rapidly thought of the names of those men who had their tiger spirits in this region. Three names came to mind and he decided to use them all rather than use only the one in case it was the wrong name. With his rifle cocked, he stepped out of the door and called out,

"Kuovi! Menuolhoulie! Wetsho! Is this the way to treat your clansman? I am Vilie, son of Kedo, your clansman. I am not here to do you harm. Why are you treating me as a stranger? I come in peace. You owe me your hospitality. I am your guest!" He shouted these words out with absolute faith that they were being listened to and heeded. Sure enough the animal retreated for the second time, but not before it had made a call like a warrior's ululating cry as it departed.

Vilie wiped away the drops of sweat that had run down his face. He had not expected to be doing anything of this sort and he didn't want to imagine how it would have gone if it had not worked. Relieved, he walked back to bed and lay down on the straw.

As he lay there – his heart still pounding loudly in his chest – he stared into the darkness struck with wonder at the fierce strangeness of the weretiger or *tekhumiavi** as theses beasts were called. The men whose spirits had metamorphosed into tigers. He remembered being told that it was by a long process that they reached their final

---

* Tekhumiavi; weretiger, the practice of transforming one's spirit into a tiger.

stage of weretigerhood. Legend said that every weretiger began as a smaller animal, possibly a wildcat. He then remembered the story of a young boy who came from a long line of weretigers. When he and his father were out hunting, a wildcat crossed their path. The boy raised his slingshot and took aim at the cat but his father knocked the slingshot from his hand. When the boy wordlessly looked at him, his father simply said, "Son, that cat is you!" That was all that the boy needed to understand that his spirit was becoming one with the tiger. He had already been told that when his spirit was metamorphosing into a tiger, it would begin with lower forms of the cat family. He was about thirteen years old, and being a sensitive young lad, knew that the wildcat would eventually grow into a mighty tiger which was his spirit.

Among the Angamis, the weretiger ritual was a closely guarded one. Men whose spirits were turning into weretigers would began to behave strangely. They would stop and stare for long periods at an object not visible to anyone else. Some men pounced on cattle and scratched them, all the while making grunting and mewling sounds. Those whose spirits had already become grown tigers gnawed on raw meat when their tigers had had a kill. The village of Dilhoma had the most number of weretigers at one point of time. But when the cattle in the village began to diminish alarmingly, the village council demanded that the men send their tigers away to another region. This was done and the cattle population was restored in the next months.

Vilie lay pondering these things for some time. It was this miracle of transformation that amazed him the most – that a man could choose to metamorphose his spirit into a tiger. He had no doubt it was true. He had heard enough stories and tonight, the way the tiger had left when he challenged his lack of courtesy, made him feel certain that there was some truth to the whole matter.

When he was growing up in the village, the elders who looked after the age-group houses,* would tell him and his companions, "It is not only the tiger that men transform themselves into. There are men in the other tribes who have been known to turn their spirits into giant snakes, and their women's spirits have become monkeys. We do not recommend these practices but we are telling you about them because knowledge is always powerful. That is what the age-group houses are for, to impart knowledge of the natural and the supernatural to you so that you go out into the world with knowledge of both, and not disrespectful of either world as some people are."

"Can you turn back into a human when you get tired of being a tiger?" one of the young men had asked.

The elder replied, "Only with great difficulty, and as though you were going through a living death. The spirit is tormented so greatly that the pain itself is a deterrent to those who want to stop being tigers."

---

* Age-group house: social institution into which children were initiated after puberty, and taught the ways of the village by an elder.

Vilie's mind brought up all that he had heard on the subject and he lay awake for several hours before exhaustion took over and he fell into a deep sleep.

SEVEN

The Nettle Forest

LIGHT FLOODED INTO THE SHED from the smashed door and shone directly upon his face. Vilie turned over and slept again. He was quite tired after the encounter with the tiger, and felt that it was more important that he got enough rest rather than press on in the state that he was in. He slept a long dreamless sleep and woke feeling drugged.

When he arose, the fire was still smouldering, and he teased the embers from the big logs until he had a flame going. He then put one of the pans on the fire and boiled some water for tea. The tiger had ruined the shed. The bamboo door hung in shreds from the hinges. Slowly drinking his tea, Vilie surveyed the damage. He got up to see if there were any tools in the shed with which he might repair the door. But there was nothing, not even a hammer. An old dao lay near the hearth, rusty and in need of sharpening. He picked it up and found a stone to whet the blade. When it was sharp enough, he cut a few bamboos, choosing to use the older plants. Vilie turned the *dao* on its blunt side and began to knock out the worst of the broken bits, and replace them as well as he could with the new bamboo. It wasn't the best repair job, nevertheless the owner would see that he had done his best with the limited means at hand.

There was nothing more he could do. With the sun rapidly rising he ate the rest of the leftover food, and hoisted his bag onto his shoulder before stepping onto the path. He quickened his pace until he was running alongside the next field. Vilie had a good idea in which direction he was headed. If he stayed on this course he would come to the waterfall, and after that, his north-westerly course would bring him to the last Zeliang villages on the border. The seer had told him he should look for two rivers. The first river was the big one but that was not the one. He should walk further until he found the smaller river, and then set up camp and wait till it went to sleep.

"Be very patient my son," the seer had said. "Only the patient-hearted are granted the blessing of catching the sleeping river."

Nobody who heard their conversation scoffed. They knew better than to do that. The seer was well versed in the things of the spiritual world, and whatever he had prophesied for the village had always come to pass.

"Take your gun with you but use it sparingly. Sometimes the struggle is not against flesh and blood, but against spiritual powers which you would be quite foolish to defy with gunpowder."

Vilie remembered the advice of the old man and repeated it to himself so that he would not miss out on any one point. He recalled the names of herbs that he should not be without, Ciena* or bitter wormwood and Tierhutiepfü,† a soft leafed plant with a rather unpleasant smell. While Ciena was good for warding off evil spirits, the other herb was supposed to be good for a number of ailments.

Vilie was a good walker and had covered a great deal more distance than he had expected from his adrenaline-fatigued body. As he came to a curve in the path he saw three figures ahead of him. They were still some distance from him but at once he became tense. The events of the night before had made him suspicious of any movements. What if this seemingly real sight metamorphosed into something else? He slowed down and carefully watched the figures, his hand on his gun.

When he drew closer he saw that there were two young girls and an older woman collecting plants that were growing abundantly in a grove.

"The Nettle Forest! Of course it is the Nettle Forest!" he muttered under his breath.

Vilie felt a bit foolish for having overlooked its location. The females were harvesting nettle which they would strip for fibre to make into yarn – it was called barkweaving. So

* Ciena: Bitter wormwood, a herb used to staunch blood from small cuts, also believed to have supernatural properties.
† Tierhutiepfii: Amaranth, a curative herb

he was not far from the village of the Barkweavers. Walking faster, he hailed the workers. They were startled as it was not often that people came by that way.

"Good day to you too," the woman returned his greeting. "Where are you headed?"

Vilie named the border village of the Zeliangs and stopped near the woman.

"Harvesting nettle?" he asked. "I didn't realise it was that time of the year already."

"It's a bit early, I admit, but it gets very hard on the hands if we wait until it is full grown. We can use these, and if dried carefully they will give us good yarn."

Vilie looked at the baskets in which they had stacked the plants after cutting off as many leaves as they could. He saw that they had pared down the stems removing the thorns along the stems. That was what they essentially needed, the long and hard, fibrous stems which they would strip lengthwise and lay in a room for a few days until the bark–fibre was ready to be wound into yarn.

Barkweaving was a dying art and it pleased him to see the women diligently harvesting the nettle plants into their baskets. The two girls had gained some expertise and he observed them as they cut the plants as close to the root as they could, and used small knives to pare off the skin so that they would not be stung in the process.

"I learnt it from my grandmother and I am trying to pass it on to my nieces," the woman spoke again.

Vilie put down his bag and his gun and sat down by

the path. It was refreshing to meet real people and have a normal conversation.

"Would you like some brew? It's quite mild," the woman offered.

Vilie was grateful for her offer and did not decline as that would have been impolite. They were many kilometres from the village. Brew was considered food and it was more or less the same as offering food to a fellow traveller. He sat there, gratefully sipping the thin rice-brew which had grains of rice floating on top. She was right. It was not strong, but it was very rich and nutritious.

EIGHT

Barkweavers

THE TWO GIRLS WORKED STEADILY at the harvesting. They did not respond to his attempts to speak to them. His questions set them giggling and Vilie didn't feel interested enough to try and converse with them.

"They don't speak your language," the woman explained. "We are Zeliang and the younger generation do not know how to speak Angami, since there was no need for them to learn it. I speak it because it was necessary in my day. Back then we traded with the Angamis and took their daos, spears and spades, and *keshiini*,* in exchange for our brine salt, pigs, dried fish and chilli. They made excellent daos because they knew how to temper steel so much better than us."

"It's a great pity that barter trading has become obsolete. Sad that the younger ones haven't learned other languages. It is always a boon to know another language," Vilie

---

* keshiini: black men's kilt, decorated with rows of white cowries

commented. "Oh I should introduce myself. I am known as Vilie, my father was Kedo, the headman of the village."

"Vilie! Surely you are the hunter who lives a solitary life in the forest near Zuzie. We have heard much about you. My husband is Keyireusap and I am Idele. My people know that you protect the tragopan."

"Has my fame travelled so far?" He smiled ironically and continued, "And you are Keyireusap's wife? What a coincidence! I know your husband but I have never had the honour of meeting you." Vilie paused but since she did not say anything, he went on. "The government pays me to see that the tragopan population does not go down in numbers, while the village uses my services to look after the *gwi* in the area. It is a good life and to be paid for living it is more than I could ask for."

"It is a brave life, I must say," Idele stated.

Vilie narrated how he had taken advantage of their hospitality having sheltered in their shed. He added that the shed had been damaged by his visitor but that he intended to pay for the damage. She smiled at the tale and said he should not bother at all as they intended to pull it down anyway, and build a new one in its place.

Idele had a broad face with high cheekbones across which the skin was tightly stretched. It was an honest face, no longer pretty but not yet wrinkled. She was in her late forties but looked older as did most of the women in the villages. Their life of hard labour aged them very fast. Her sunburnt fingers deftly held the knife with its blade close to the very base of the plants as she cut them, and removed just enough bark to enable her to tie the plants together without damaging the rest.

"Nettle is good in broths too," she said, feeling his eyes upon her.

"Yes, I have heard that," Vilie replied. "Do you think I could try that?" he asked.

"Try what? Harvesting nettle? Of course." She handed him her knife and as an afterthought tossed him a thick pad of cloth which hung on her waist-belt.

"Here, use this pad, accidents can happen the first time and nettle stings can linger a long time."

Vilie took the cloth and fumbled a bit. Idele took the cloth from him and showed him how to cover a bit of the stem so he could cut it without getting stung. When he tried cutting it, the nettle plant stubbornly held on. Growing impatient Vilie yanked the plant out and got stung for his troubles. "Damn!" he swore and let go of the plant. Idele knew what had happened and quickly looked around for an antidote. She plucked the leaves off a small bitter wormwood plant and kneaded it to pulp in her hand. Then she handed it over to Vilie.

"Damn! That was more painful than the nettle we have in the village, is it another variety? "

"It's stronger than the species found in your area. It yields better yarn but it stings harder too," Idele explained.

Vilie kept rubbing the paste into his skin, and that seemed to ease the smarting.

"Sorry, I thought you would know." They looked at each other and Vilie gave a rueful smile.

"That was as good a signal as any that I should be on my way," he said.

"Wait, I will give you something else to put on it." She reached into her bag and brought forth a small bottle with a cork-stopper.

"What is it?" Vilie asked.

"Rock bee honey," Idele replied, "It's a cure-all. Let's get some on your wound." Without waiting for an answer she smeared honey generously over the swelling skin and covered it with a leaf.

"You want to be careful with that," she said." If you are not used to it, this variety of nettle can give you a nasty little fever."

"I'll be all right," he insisted.

"Rest a while and then go when the swelling subsides. I mean it."

So Vilie sat down by the path again and waited. The honey counteracted against the sting by making his skin sore so that the bitter stinging was somewhat reduced. It felt much better.

"Will you weave me a nettle cloth?" he said impulsively. "I will come back by this way and can even come to your village and collect it. I will pay for it of course."

"It would be an honour to weave you a cloth. We are always weaving nettle cloths when the yarn is spun. It's good to use it in season. It is still called bark-cloth by the old people."

"Bark-cloth, I will remember that," Vilie said solemnly as he rose to go.

He took leave of them and went on his way. At the turning in the road, he looked back and waved at them. He thought he saw a half-wave.

Company for the Night

VILIE PICKED UP SPEED when he was clear of the Nettle Forest. The nettles grew on either side of the path so if he missed his footing he would have fallen into the shrubbery and gotten a nasty surprise. He was understandably quite relieved when he reached the end of the forest. The Nettle Forest was not as big an area as its name would suggest. It was less than half a kilometre, and the nettles grew very high – some as tall as trees in the heart of the forest. Those had never been harvested as it was impossible to pass through the thick growth to get to them. So they had grown unhindered until they reached their present height. People who had never seen the nettle-trees scoffed at such a thing. But those who had been to the Nettle Forest knew better.

Vilie still had some five hours of daylight, and he meant to make the most of it. He habitually walked with long strides, and others found it difficult to keep up with him. It was a good thing he travelled alone most of the time, a friend once teased him. Vilie was not very tall, but he was a lean man and that gave the impression of height. He had a rather prominently hooked nose and it made him appear stern. But that was far from the truth. The guardian of the forest carefully tended to injured forest dwellers when he came across them on his walks through the forest. He was skilled at using splints to set broken bones. He would make pastes of ciena for open wounds. That worked for smaller injuries, but for bigger wounds he liked to use the pungent *Japan nha** and rock bee honey. He had tried these on himself, and the healing had been quick, with little scarring.

After a couple of hours, he reached the next valley and was debating whether or not to set up camp for the night when he heard voices ahead. It was a small group of hunters. He shouted out to them. The four men stopped and waited for him to catch up.

"Not alone, are you?" asked the leader of the group, a grizzled old man.

"I'm on my own," Vilie answered.

"Oh that's not safe in these parts," said the old man.

"I know these lands," Vilie spoke up quickly. The other three men were standing at a distance and Vilie raised his hand to them by way of salutation. They shouted back greetings.

"We are planning to camp at the base of the peak," their leader explained. "You can join us if you want."

---

* japan nha: Crofton weed.

Vilie accepted the offer gratefully. There was safety in numbers and he was happy for the unexpected company. They walked together for another four hours until they were directly under the shadow of the peak. The sun had set and they hastily chopped wood and cut elephant grass to make a shelter. The men were carrying dried fish, and when the fire was made they roasted the fish and ground it into *tathu.* They would not let Vilie use up his rations, insisting that he would have greater need for them later.

After their meal, Vilie felt drowsy and laid his head on a rock. When he had rested a bit, he felt that it was very impolite to go to sleep without exchanging some conversation with his hosts. So he roused himself and filled his mug with red tea.

The other three in the group were from the same family. Three brothers. They were occasional hunters who were after the wild boar that had been seen headed this way after ravaging some fields of maize. The youngest of the trio was only nineteen. He said he had once shot a bear, but didn't get to kill it.

"Did you see the animal up close?" Vilie asked.

"Not exactly, but he was big and brown and grunted when I shot at him from the back," answered the young man whose name was Abu.

Vilie refrained from remarking that it perhaps was not a bear but a wild pig. The second brother was about 25 and

---

* tathu: a savoury side dish of pounded chilli, dried fish or meat, roasted tomatoes, with garlic or ginger.

had more experience of hunting. He didn't seem to be as friendly as his younger brother. Vilie heard them calling him Manhie. The oldest was 32 and was the heaviest of the three. He took swigs from a flask of whisky that he carried and was a bit gregarious.

"We should turn in early," said the leader whose name was Pehu.

The plan for the next day was to find trees where the animals were feeding. Then they would stay up the night waiting in turns for their prey. But the oldest of the three brothers was reluctant to leave his drinking.

"Enough of that, Hiesa, you won't be able to shoot straight when an animal comes," Pehu stated in a firm tone. "Get to bed now, otherwise you will have a terrible hangover tomorrow."

"All we've done is walk all day. I want to have some fun too!" Hiesa protested.

"Look, you are not going to be in any condition to hunt if you get so wasted now. Off to bed with you, you great lump of lard."

"Don't call me names now, you hear," Hiesa's tone was belligerent.

"Ok, ok just get to bed then and sleep off your drunkenness."

Vilie said a hurried goodnight and crept into a tent and lay on the grass-covered mound that was going to be his bed for the night. He crawled under his blanket and tried to sleep.

TEN

Under Cover of Darkness

VILIE WASN'T SURE how long he lay awake. The two men outside were arguing loudly. At first Vilie thought they would calm down but they did not. All of a sudden he had a premonition that things were not going to end well. It made him tense. He did not ignore the feeling because that was something he was familiar with from before. His mind began to work automatically. Pack your things, get out of here, it commanded. He did not hesitate. He had gathered up his blanket and was stuffing it into his bag when the loud retort of a gun went off, followed by a man's strangled cry and then silence. Vilie grabbed his gun and sprang to his feet. He was not imagining things. That gunshot had been loud enough to wake the dead. The two younger men were still snoring in their sleep on the other side of the shelter, and Vilie had chosen to lie next to the opening. Surely they would wake up with the noise.

Very cautiously, Vilie crept to the edge of the shelter and

peered out. By the light of the fire, he could see that one man was hunched over and not moving. The other figure was hulked over him, still holding the gun with which he had shot his companion. Between sobs, Hiesa was saying, "I told you to shut up but you wouldn't listen, I told you, I told you."

Pehu was not moving at all. Vilie debated what to do, should he go out and try to take the gun from Hiesa? Or should he pretend to be asleep and let the other two deal with things? The two brothers were stirring in their sleep, woken by the gunshot. As Vilie dithered, Hiesa became aware of him. He swung his gun in Vilie's direction and called out, "Who is it? Who's there?"

Vilie was not sure if the man would try to shoot him too. Grabbing his bag and gun, he ran madly out of the shelter, zigzagging his way across the fields. He heard Hiesa roar in anger and a bullet was shot in his direction. It whizzed past him. Vilie ran like he had never run before. He knew that if he slowed down, Hiesa would shoot him dead. He could outrun him and he had to hope that the man's aim was not good from a distance. More bullets followed. One had grazed his arm but he felt nothing. Vilie ran headlong into the forest, running until his breath in his throat hurt him. The shouting voice grew dimmer and stopped altogether. He ran until he could run no more. He shored up against a tree, but his legs were shaking violently and his knees buckled beneath him. He didn't feel safe enough to stop, so he went on all fours and began to crawl along the forest floor, his bag under his belly and his gun on his back.

The thought of going back and sorting things out was not an option now. He knew he should get away as far as he could from that madman with the gun. He thought he heard the others shouting but could not be sure. Crawling, resting a little, crawling again, he slowly calmed down and regained some strength. He quickly decided to change course. If they were occasional hunters, they would know the area and its possible hiding places well. They could predict the direction in which he was headed. Vilie's decision took all that into account. He would not follow the path to its destination which was the village of Hinema. He would detour even further east on a north-easterly direction and hope that he would arrive at the border villages at some point.

He stopped to check that nothing had fallen out of his bag. He then swung his bag on his back, picked up his gun and turned further into the woods. Now he was walking and half running very far from the path that ran for miles through the forest. Vilie had come this way only once with his uncle, a veteran hunter. He hoped he would remember the landmarks. There were more trees now but he still felt it would be dangerous to stop for long to check if he was going the right way. After many hours, the track he had chosen led him to a region where very tall trees grew with foliage that covered the sky from view. It looked like the forest called *Rarhuria*,* the unclean forest. He was quite lost by now but at least he knew that if he kept heading northeast from here he would arrive at the border between Manipur and Nagaland. He clung to that knowledge.

* Rarhuria: unclean forest, certain spirit-infested places shunned by villagers.

ELEVEN

The Forest was His Wife

ONLY WHEN HE WAS in the heart of the rainforest did Vilie feel safe. He found a fig tree to rest beneath. With trembling hands he pulled out his tobacco pouch and stopped when he saw blood congealed on his arm. It was from the bullet that had grazed him while he was running. The wound was superficial but now it was beginning to throb. I'll tend to that later, he thought and rolled a smoke. Inhaling deeply, he calmed down and thought of his new situation. A man had been killed and he had run from the scene. How long would it take for the villagers to find out about the killing? The three hunters were brothers. Very likely they would stick to the same story. And then what? Call it an accident? Surely not. Yet surely they would not try to blame it on him? His heart missed a beat. That was something he had not considered. He had been so intent upon not being shot that he had run further into the forest and not toward the village. Should he change direction now and head to his ancestral village to tell them what had really happened?

Vilie considered that thought carefully. They were from different villages and murder was an inter-village affair.

He rejected the idea of approaching the Dichu village where Pehu and Hiesa hailed from. It did not seem like a practical idea at all. How could his story be accepted above the version of the three brothers? How could he be sure they were not still looking for him trying to kill him? It was too big a risk to take. That made up his mind for him. He felt clear about some things. Hide here for some days until he was sure they had given up looking for him. Then walk back to his own village, Zuzie, and find his clansmen and get their help with the problem. He could not represent himself but they could and they would do it willingly. Of course he knew that he should not stay away too long. As soon as it was safe he would find his way back to Zuzie, explain the matter, and let them take it from there. The problem was that to get back to Zuzie, he would have to cross Dichu territory until he got to the bridge that divided their land from Zuzie. There was no way around it. He would simply have to be as quiet and unobtrusive as possible.

There was a movement on the ground. Squirrels running up and down a tree. He didn't have the heart to kill them for food so he looked around to see if there were any herbs. Finding a patch of *Vilhuü nha*,* he made a paste out of the leaves and stuck it on his injury and let the brown juice seep into his open skin. The bleeding stopped immediately.

---

* Vilhuii nha:Redflower ragleaf, or Fireweed, medicinal herb.

On the branches of the tree he was resting beneath were stalks of *jotho*[*] the soft-stalked herb that could be added to almost any broth. He decided he would first make a shelter and then gather some *jotho* for his pot. There were also young *gara*[†] and *gapa*[‡] plants at the base of the tree. He would not want for food here.

Vilie made a hasty shelter with the large leaves that seemed to be constantly falling from the trees. They fell with mighty crashing sounds that the forest magnified. The ground was moss-covered, so he gathered leaves to make a bed as well. This would hopefully keep out the moisture that seeped up from the ground. Having built himself a small shelter, he sought a place to make a small smokeless fire. That was something every good hunter knew. If leaves are laid over a fire in a thick layer, the smoke will never travel up and betray your presence.

Into his pot went the herbs he had shredded into small pieces, along with salt and rice. A piece of dried meat would add just exactly the flavour he needed. When the meat was tender, Vilie waited for the food to cool. His gun by his side, he ate slowly, always peering past the trees so no one would come upon him by surprise. He needn't have been afraid. The rainforest was shunned by both villagers and local hunters alike. It was indeed the *Rarhuria*, the unclean forest feared by all who knew of it.

---

[*] Jotho: edible species of the nettle family.

[†] Gara: Indian pennywort.

[‡] Gapa: Great plantain.

The interior of the forest was dark and dank. Those who unknowingly wandered into the *Rarhuria* complained of fever and headaches afterwards. There were enough cases of fever to warrant labelling the rainforest an unclean area in village terminology. People studiously avoided coming near the forest.

But for Vilie this was a boon. He could recoup his strength here and try to make his way back. After eating, he took a long walk and then circled back to his shelter and assured himself no one had followed him. On his return, he felt safe enough to stretch out under his leafy roof. The forest was his wife indeed: providing him with sanctuary when he most needed it; and food when his rations were inadequate. The forest also protected him from the evil in the heart of man. He felt truly wedded to her at this moment.

TWELVE

Fever

VILIE SLEPT THROUGH THE NIGHT but woke just before
dawn with a loud pounding in his temples that would not
go away. He was sweating and felt uncomfortably warm.
He threw off his blanket thinking that the temperature had
suddenly risen toward morning. But it wasn't that. When
the wind blew in, it was cool and soothed his moist skin.
There was no humidity in the atmosphere. Vilie realised
he had contracted a fever. That was why his head was
pulsating, and keeping him awake. He struggled to his feet
to find water to drink. The night before, he had heard the
tinkling of water so he knew there was a stream nearby –
possibly quite close for he had heard it quite distinctly.
He went out and tried to listen again. The tinkling came
further down from his shelter. Vilie walked down to the
small stream and filled his water canteen. He splashed
some water on his face, trying to clear what seemed like
cobwebs in his head. Then he straggled back to the shelter.
The water hadn't really helped. He had aches in his joints

and it was an effort to sit up. He collapsed onto the leaf-mound.

Vilie wasn't sure how long he stayed like that. He regained consciousness when a big branch fell from a tree with a loud crash. It roused him and he struggled to the fire, teased it till it gave some flames to warm his tea water. He wasn't sure what was happening but he had no strength left even to walk to the next tree. Drinking his partially warmed tea, he groped for his tobacco. It was damp and difficult to drag. When the nicotine hit him, he coughed and choked alternately.

"Damn! What's wrong with me?" he swore and put out the smoke.

He had never reacted like that to tobacco before. Today it was just too strong for him. He felt that he could no longer abide the smell of native tobacco in his nostrils. Vilie crawled into bed and was overcome by sleep.

The fever lasted two whole days and nights. Throughout, he perspired heavily and had an unquenchable thirst. He would drag himself to the stream, fill his canteen and return. After a while, he was so tired he simply drank water straight from the canteen without bothering to boil it.

Vilie drifted in and out of sleep, waking up only long enough to turn over and go to sleep again. It felt like a malarial fever and it left him weak when it finally left him. He thought of the people from his village who used to fall sick when they wandered into the *Rarhuria* while out hunting or cutting wood. To cure them the seer would give them a drink made of ginseng and *tsomhou*,* the wild sour seed that grew on trees. Stir in a little honey and the mixture would go down easily. But Vilie had none of these with him and decided that the only thing to do was to wait it out. In any case, he had no energy to do otherwise. He did not know these woods so he did not whether these curative herbs were to be found here.

A hundred years ago, the non-Christians customarily offered chicken sacrifices if anyone fell sick. They feared death so much that they would bring a chicken into the woods and proclaim, "Life for life" and release the chicken so that it cheeped all evening until it died or was eaten by a bigger animal. But no one did that now because the Christians taught that *Jisu* had been sacrificed for everyone's sickness so nobody needed to offer chicken sacrifices again. Vilie's thoughts lingered on the chicken sacrifice, and he wished he could have some chicken broth to strengthen him. He was very weak from the fever and lack of food. He turned over and fell asleep again, helpless as a baby.

---

* Tsomhou: nutgall tree.

THIRTEEN

"You Can Eat Yourself Dead!"

THE MORNING OF THE THIRD DAY, the fever left him. When he woke, the pounding in his head was gone. He tried sitting up and managed to sit for some minutes without wanting to lie back on the ground. Not surprisingly, he also felt amazingly hungry. Pulling himself out of bed, he made a new fire because the old one had gone cold. Bringing the water to a boil, he quickly put in salt and rice and added bits of dried meat. When he set out he had no doubt he would be able to replenish his diet with fresh meat every now and again. But that had not happened and now he was running short of dried meat. But that was not the biggest of his worries. Getting stronger and finding his way back to the village was where he needed to focus his energies.

Vilie ate slowly, because that was what he had always been taught. All hunters knew that if they found food after a long period of starvation, they should eat slowly, masticating their food properly to help their digestive organs. "You can eat yourself dead!" the older hunters would warn when they were teaching younger hunters about this. They were very serious about it.

Vilie felt the strength return to his limbs and wondered at that little miracle. The simple act of eating food had given him new energy and he felt all the tiredness of the previous days disappearing. He was ravenously hungry but he paced himself and ate small portions, chewing slowly and deliberately. Vilie must have taken a whole hour to finish his meal as he ate and rested, and ate and rested again. But it did him good. His mother used to say that food eaten slowly stayed in your stomach longer. He trusted the wisdom of that.

Should he rest another day and make the trip tomorrow? The thought was tempting. Vilie knew he was safe in the forest. If the brothers were still looking for him, he would not be able to outrun them a second time in the state that he was in. His body was telling him he was not ready yet and he wanted to listen to his body. He would spend another night in the *Rarhuria* and make the trip in the morning.

It was a good decision. All day he alternated between resting and eating small meals. He added herbs to his pot and felt nourished by the green forest leaves which he ate partially cooked. As the day drew on he climbed one of the trees to get above the foliage, and see if there were any people around outside the *Rarhuria*. He could not see anyone for miles around. Feeling safe he climbed down and walked a bit, stretching his legs and feeling the muscles groan at the exercise. It was good to walk on the mossy forest floor. Not only was it gentle on his feet, he felt it was gentle on his muscles, and the walking helped build them up without straining them.

When he came back to the shelter, he picked up his tobacco pouch and started to roll a smoke. But the pungent smell of native tobacco wafting up was still distasteful to him. It made him feel nauseous and the desire to smoke left him. How strange! He had been a smoker all his adult life and this had never happened to him before. Could it be that his body was too weakened by fever? Native tobacco was quite strong after all. It was stronger than the shop cigarettes and left his mouth numb if he smoked too much. It seemed like he was going off it. The thought made him laugh a bit. Ah, maybe it was just as well. One thing that gave away a hunter's presence to animals was tobacco smoke. Wild animals could smell tobacco smoke from a long distance away. He tossed the half rolled smoke into the fire and regretted it at once. Black smoke instantly mushroomed upward and since he couldn't move quickly enough, he inhaled some of it. He coughed and coughed. His throat was burning as he ran to the stream and sluiced it with cool water. Ha! Never again would he do that. Staying as far from the smoke as he could, he poked at the butt and pushed it away from the smouldering logs so the rest of it would burn out.

FOURTEEN

The Backward Route

VILIE WOKE BEFORE DAWN, gathered his things into his bag, and packed the remnants of the previous night's meal in a leaf for later use. He was stronger and quite ready now for the long trip back. He doused his fire and stamped out the few embers that stubbornly tried to burn in spite of the dousing. Carefully tracing his way out of the forest, Vilie emerged at a spot from where he could see a narrow but well beaten track. If he stayed on it, his chances of getting to the base of the hill where he had met the hunters were better. He would still have to look out for the hunters and walk stealthily among the trees beside the track.

He made very slow progress, because he had to stop every time he heard a sound up ahead. The track was deserted but Vilie did not want to proceed until he had surveyed what lay ahead. He kept well out of sight, running from tree to tree or grove to grove and catching his breath before the next sprint. It was exhausting. When evening came, he was disappointed to see he had not covered much ground at all. But what could he do except continue in that manner? It would be safer now that the light was going and visibility was poor. He would not be able to see very well in front of him, but the fact that reassured him was that those chasing him would not be able to recognise him if they sighted him. Armed with this thought, he walked more boldly along the track and covered much more distance before he camped for the night.

Vilie had run so far off course that he no longer recognised the terrain he was traversing. But he knew that if he went in the direction opposite to the one he had been following he would come to a path that veered off to his ancestral village. Perhaps he would reach it in another two days if he could set a faster pace. Since he was not sure of the route back, he felt the urge to camp for the night before it turned completely dark. That placed him in another dilemma. He no longer dared camp in the open. The sheds in the fields that he would normally have chosen were not an option now. Those were the first places they would look. So it was back to making a quick shelter for the night and dismantling it in the morning so that no trace of it would be left for them to track him down.

When he lay down to rest, he was suddenly filled with a great wave of sympathy for all creatures that had ever been in the situation that he found himself in now. So this was how they felt – the fugitives on the run from other men, both the guilty and the innocent – a cringing fear of all men and all signs of human dwelling. He had never experienced this before. It was unusual to feel this way. He felt somewhat guilty and tried to shrug off the feeling. Why should he feel guilty when he had not done anything wrong? He did not foresee that the quarrelling would end in murder. But why hadn't he intervened before it went wrong? If the two of them had insisted that Hiesa go to sleep, they would have been in the majority, and Hiesa would have had to listen to them. Ah, but there was no point in thinking about all that now. What was done was done. Now the important thing was to set things straight before they got too far out of control.

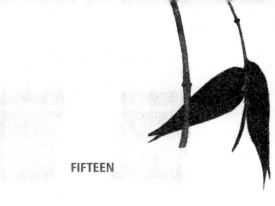

FIFTEEN

Posse

VILIE WOKE BEFORE IT WAS LIGHT. That was fine with him. The more distance he could cover before daylight, the better off he would be. So he was on his way and got clear of the track by the time the sun came up. From then on, it was three low hills to cross before the forest paths converged into one that led to the village. It was safer, but it was also hard going because he had to climb the steep face of the first hill just to avoid detection.

The first hill was the steepest: hard, jutting rock throughout, with barely any vegetation on it. Vilie crouched and crawled up the rock face at the base of the hill. Roots of trees and shrubs gave him handholds, but it was difficult and untested so it was dangerous. He tried each hold two or three times before trusting it with his body-weight. If a shrub seemed as though it could not take his weight, he let go of it and tried another. Should it not hold, he would go tumbling down the slope, and risk breaking his bones upon the rocks below. After the first section, it got better and he came to a spot where the rocks hid him from view. Vilie paused at that section, and laid his bag and gun down while he sat down and rested. He drank some water from his canteen and lay on the grass. It was cool and pleasant, for the hard climb had made him sweat profusely.

Could he take another round of climbing? Feeling rested and ready, Vilie got up and started walking again. The trail went up and then went round the west side which was quite rocky, and a wrong step could end in a fatal fall. There were no edges or shrubs to hold on this side, and though it was a short distance, it was incredibly narrow. The safest way to cross was to plaster oneself to the rock wall and slide across. Luckily it was not a long stretch at all, and Vilie could breathe a big sigh of relief when he had crossed it. He felt the fatigue in his wrists and forearms, but he could rest again – aided by the shade of rocks and shrubbery. He stretched himself out behind the rocks and looked upward. The sky was a deep clear blue dotted with clouds, and for long moments he stared at that peaceful sight. It almost made him forget why he was there.

Vilie must have taken nearly three hours to climb the first hill. On the descent he was relieved to find thick vegetation again. It afforded him the cover he so dearly craved. The sun was high in the sky when he reached the second hill. Spurred on by his first success, he ran up the hill. It was not rocky like the first hill nor was it as steep, but it was plateau-like on the top with hardly any trees growing on it. Thick clumps of elephant grass grew in several spots. The grass was as tall as Vilie or taller. From afar an observant eye could still see that someone was moving amidst the grass. Vilie was aware of this and tried to move as slowly as possible. He hoped that if he was spotted, they would think it was only the wind making the grass sway. The whole length of the plateau-top was covered by elephant grass. The track that ran between the growths of grass was pressed down and obviously well-trodden. Possibly there was a risk of running into other people here. The long walk came to an end when he reached the slope. After that he came to the valley, and he was soon standing in front of the third hill. He climbed the hillock undetected and rested near the summit.

Before he began the descent, Vilie stopped and found a good vantage point where he could survey the valley. He could see a few figures that were not clearly distinguishable. He waited for them to come closer and looked again. This time he could count the six men who were walking in a line in his direction. He saw that some of them carried guns. Who were they? Hunters? Would it be safe for him to encounter them?

Dark Heart of Man

VILIE WAITED FOR A LONG TIME before he climbed down the hill. By then the sun had set, and when he reached the valley it was quite dark, and only the silhouettes of the trees were visible. The men he had seen from atop the hillock continued to march in his direction. He was still unsure what he should do. His eyes sought out tall trees to climb and hide in. But there were no tall trees to be found, so the only option he had was to lie very quiet in a thick bush and hope they would not find him. He found a copse of thorn bushes and cowered there. With some luck, he should be able to avoid capture.

The men came closer into the small cleave of the valley. Now he could hear their voices and discern what they were saying for they were talking loudly.

"If we fail to catch him, we cannot till our fields in safety. No man or woman will be free from ambush."

A second voice burst in, "We should lynch him when he is caught – an eye for an eye."

There was anger in the voices and fear. Vilie could not make out every word that they said, but it was clear this was a mob out to administer justice without any mercy. They circled the woods angrily in their search for him. Some of them spoke in the dialect of Hiesa's village and there were some men who spoke in another dialect. They were a mixed bunch. They carried torches and guns, and they began to light the torches so that the surrounding areas were well lit up. They knew that this time of evening offered the most shelter to a fugitive, especially when the night was fast darkening the valley. The men went this way and that, always in twos and never far from each other. Vilie realised that if he made a run for it, they would not hesitate to shoot him. They began shouting again, one saying they should have brought the dogs and another saying the killer couldn't run away forever.

Suddenly Vilie heard one of the men say, "There will be no lynching without a trial. We are not savages. We will conduct a trial."

"What's the good of a trial? He shot an unarmed man without giving him any chance to defend himself. Why should we show him any mercy?" said another.

The first man spoke again in a firm and hard voice,

"Listen to me! I insist there will be no lynching without a trial. I will not hesitate to shoot anyone who tries to take the law into his own hands." Something about the voice sounded very familiar to Vilie. He was sure he had heard it before.

"Teiso, do you mean we are just going to throw away the four days we have searched for the killer?" asked the second speaker defiantly.

"I won't repeat myself," said the man called Teiso. He spoke with authority.

Teiso, Teiso, it must be Teiso Yhokha! Vilie thought quickly. He knew the man and had met him briefly when he came to his part of the forest looking for *gwi*. Vilie had not dared to peer at the men but when he heard Teiso's voice, he inched forward and by the light of the torches, saw that indeed it was Teiso Yhokha. Rapidly thinking things through, and not dwelling too long on it in case he changed his mind, Vilie stepped out into the open shouting, "Don't shoot, here I am, you can take me prisoner!"

That caught them completely by surprise. Guns were swiftly cocked and pointed at him. "Don't shoot," he repeated, "Here's my gun." So saying he slid his gun on the ground in their direction.

"Step forward slowly," said the man closest to him. His gun was aimed straight at Vilie's heart.

"I can explain," Vilie began to say.

"Shut up! Don't say a word until you are told to," ordered the man who had been arguing with Teiso.

Vilie came forward with his hands upraised. He tried to walk as calmly as possible. He didn't want to provoke this trigger-happy lot.

"Stop there, I say stop! Hands on your head!"

Vilie stood completely still with his hands above his head. The men came forward cautiously with their torches and guns. One boldly brought his torch close to Vilie's face.

"It is him," he said triumphantly, "look at that scar on his cheek." The man held the torch so close to Vilie's face that he felt the heat on his cheek but he dared not protest. Like a hunted animal he was circled by the other men. In turns, they peered at his scar and stared hard at him, and tightened their circle.

Mercifully, the torch was withdrawn when the torchbearer's attention was drawn to Vilie's bag. He prodded at it roughly.

"Put the bag down!" he said loudly.

Vilie slipped the bag onto the ground and one man grabbed it and overturned its contents.

"Bullets!" shouted the man who was going through it. The butt of a rifle smashed into Vilie's back. He let out a painful grunt and fell forward.

Teiso Yhokha stepped up and said, "That's enough! Put the things back into his bag. And you, sit down with your hands on your head," this last he addressed to Vilie.

Vilie sat down without saying a word. He hoped Teiso had recognised him. He didn't try to say anything in case it made the others pounce on him again.

"Make sure he's not carrying any concealed weapons!" ordered Teiso and the man with the torch did a thorough search of Vilie. They bound his hands behind him, and the rope cut into his wrists. Vilie let them do what they wanted. At this stage any resistance on his part would be stupid, and would only provoke more violent treatment.

SEVENTEEN

Jungle Justice

VILIE SPENT THE NIGHT TRUSSED up like a pig. They had
bound him hand and foot and the bound areas turned numb
after some hours. In a way he was grateful for the numbness,
because the pain from muscles and sinews that were
stretched in an unnatural manner was almost unbearable.
They spent the night in the valley and his captors slept in
turns – though he had no intention of running away when
he had given himself up. He was bound so tightly that escape
was impossible. When it grew a little light the men roused
themselves and they cut a sturdy pole and strung him up.
Taking turns they carried him back with them.

However, they did not take him all the way back to the
village. They were met on the way by a group of the village
elders. The men set him down on the ground.

"Have you questioned him?" the leader asked the men.

"Not yet," Teiso Yhokha replied.

"Loosen his bonds. A man cannot talk trussed up like
a chicken."

His bonds were loosened and he could now stretch his limbs. A muffled grunt escaped him from the pain of the blood flowing again through his numbed limbs. He rubbed his wrists weakly, trying to rub the soreness out of them.

One of the elders sent a flask of tea around to his captors. Someone handed him a mug of tea. He took it and sipped slowly.

Vilie had stopped thinking about the wisdom of giving himself up. He hoped his faith in Teiso Yhokha would not be shaken. Teiso had not acknowledged him. Perhaps that was just as well if he were to help him getting a trial. The others would probably think that Teiso was being biased if they found out that the two of them were known to each other. The elders sat lined up before him, and his captors positioned themselves behind him, and two of them sat on either side of him to prevent his escape. They still had their guns at the ready in case he should try anything.

"What is your name?" the questioning began. What is your clan? Where is your ancestral village? What are you doing in these parts? Were you known to Pehu of Dichu village? Why were you in his company? Do you deny that you argued with him and shot him dead and then ran off from the camp he had so graciously shared with you? The questioning was cleverly done. There was room only for monosyllabic or one line answers. But at the end of it, the elder said he would be given the opportunity to present his side of the case.

Vilie cleared his throat and began to address them.

First he thanked them for not killing him straight away. Choosing his words carefully he told them how he had been travelling toward the border villages when the incident happened. He looked at the faces around him. Some of them looked interested and the others simply looked stern. Vilie suddenly stopped speaking and took off his jacket. He pushed up his shirt sleeve.

"If you don't believe me, look that's where the second bullet grazed my arm."

The wound was red and showed signs that it had festered and was slowly drying up. Teiso held his arm to the light and examined it.

"He is speaking the truth, this is a wound made by a bullet from a .22 rifle. I can vouch for that. Hiesa uses just such a rifle. Further, I want you to consider that we found this man walking in the direction of the village. A common fugitive would not walk toward the village where he would surely be captured. He would be far from here if he were running from capture."

There was a gasp and confusion broke out amongst his captors, but the elder called for silence. The loud voices gradually lowered their arguing to murmuring and then the elder shouted for silence again. They let him speak.

"Teiso Yhokha is an experienced hunter and an expert on guns. He has no profit to make by siding with a killer, if this man has indeed killed Pehu. If we are to disregard this evidence and lynch this man in spite of his innocence, we will reap the punishment of our wrong actions. This man is known to the community here by reputation. He is the guardian of the forest in the western areas of the tragopan. I have heard of him. All that has been said about him in the neighbouring villages have been good reports, whereas Hiesa, our clansman, is known to all as a lover of drink and a belligerent, quarrelsome man. I would accept Teiso's testimony over Hiesa's version."

The listening men began to murmur amongst themselves again. This time the elder did not stop them. Rather unexpectedly, the man who had hit Vilie with the butt of his rifle came up to him.

"If I have made a mistake in hitting you, I hope you will not hold that against me."

He couldn't look Vilie in the face. Vilie reached a hand out and squeezed the man's arm. He was just so relieved that the elder had accepted Teiso Yhokha's verdict, and he didn't want to hold any grudges against his captors. Was he free to go now? He wondered but hesitated to ask.

Almost reading his thoughts, the elder turned to him,

"You are free to go. We deeply regret you were roughly treated by some of our men. I want to offer to take you home to my house and treat your wounds and give you provisions for your journey."

Vilie declined the offer as politely as he could. He did not want to be in the same village as Hiesa who had tried to kill him. He would continue to use herbs on his wound and proceed on his way once he got back on course. And he would make sure he avoided the company of humans. That was one clear thought on his mind. The men of Dichu were apologetic and even offered to give him food and medicinal herbs, but the only thing on his mind was to get away from them as quickly as possible. Thankfully, they did not press him.

"May this not come between us and your people, O guardian of the forest," the elder said. Vilie nodded at him but had no words to answer him.

He was given back his gun and bag. Vilie gathered up these and said his farewells hastily, and retraced his steps back on the way he had come.

As he was walking away Vilie inclined his head at Teiso Yhokha. It was a very slight motion, almost imperceptible. They did not exchange a single word. Both silently assented that it was wisest if they kept the group ignorant of their acquaintance. In a few hours, Vilie was very far from the wayside shed where his fate had been decided.

EIGHTEEN

Back on Track

AFTER LEAVING THE MEN BEHIND, Vilie felt he was back on track – back on the mission from which he had been so efficiently derailed. He must try to travel alone from now on. Of course, he had not had the slightest inkling that accepting the offer of the hunters would end so badly. Not only had he lost time, he was way off course. But the good thing about the whole incident (if it could even be put that way) was that he had got his bearings back. Determined not to be distracted this time, Vilie quickened his pace. Only a short time had passed when he found himself at a crossroads. There were multiple paths leading off in different directions, making it difficult to choose which one to take. He decided on the path that looked the least trodden. It led away from the other paths people frequently used, to walk to and from the western villages.

Vilie slowed down his pace and as he did so, the pain returned to his bruised wrists which had been twisted behind him and tied. His ankles were sore where he had been trussed up on the pole while they carried him to the village shed. He had not noticed the pain when he first set out, because his mind was so focused on putting distance between himself and the men who had wanted to lynch him. He had created that distance now but when he allowed himself to relax, he felt as if needles were being jabbed into his calf muscles and thighs. A debilitating, dull throbbing soreness followed the jabbing, making it increasingly difficult for him to walk without a limp.

The course he was following would lead him back onto the route he had used before he met the hunting group. It was slow going with frequent rests where he rubbed his ankles to get the blood flowing properly. The tingling soreness in his ankles slowed him down. He had no salve with him, so stopping and rubbing on the sore places was all he could do to ease the pain a little. He limped as he tried to avoid putting pressure on his sore ankles. The right thing to do would have been to rest for a couple of days, feeding on chicken soup and country ginger to heal his injuries. Chicken meat was no good if you had a fever or an open wound, but it was always good for other injuries, and besides, it was his wrists and ankles hurting him, not so much the bullet wound which had congealed before forming pus.

He was very close to *Rarhuria* now. But there was no fear of the unclean forest in him now. Strange. In the old days he – and indeed all the villagers – would have had nothing to do with the unclean forest. The old men and old

women in particular persistently warned children to avoid
it entirely. They said it was the place where human children
were taken away by spirit children who appeared before
them and engaged them in play. The human children would
go missing for days and no search party could find them
until the spirit children tired of their play and released
their new friends. The old women had many stories to tell
of the children who were found again. They never seemed
any the worse for their escapades. They would say they had
been playing a very nice game and been fed berries, roots
and even worms.

Men, especially when out hunting, swore they had
seen beautiful long-haired girls playing and singing to
each other in the forest. That was why they called them
forest songs. A forest song was a spirit song sung very
melodiously and could be heard by a lone hunter, and also
by a group of people such as an age-group. The old men
said that the spirits used forest songs to enchant humans,
and draw them to the unclean forest so they would die and
come to live with them there. Vilie had never heard a forest
song but one of his age-mates had. He had recounted it
to their mates in the age-group house at night when they
were all sitting together by the fire.

"It's beautiful, beautiful, and they sing such haunting
melodies the like I have never heard before. Nothing near
the age-group songs that we think are so excellent. Their
songs are not sung loudly but they wend their way into
your brain and stay there lulling you and drawing you out

of yourself with the incredible sweetness. That's what it is! They sing such sweet songs that you want to cry when they stop because you want nothing other than to keep on listening."

Vilie had not been very interested back then because he was not one for singing, certainly not the heavy folk songs that his age-group were so fond of singing at festivals – dragging back and forth the folk anthems like a weight between groups of male and female singers sitting across from each other, dressed in their festival best. Nevertheless he had been fascinated with the stories of the unclean forest and its spirit inhabitants. He was entering the unclean forest now and it felt different from the last time he had been there. It was late evening and the canopy made by the tree branches had thrown the interior of the forest into further darkness.

Vilie found a big tree he could shelter beneath, and he quickly gathered branches to make a leafy roof for the night. He piled leaves atop moss to make a bed and gathered twigs to make a fire. As he was working on the shelter, the light was rapidly departing. He made haste to make a big fire and proceeded to collect firewood by its light. It was not very prudent and he reminded himself that he should always gather firewood first before making a shelter. The result was that some of the logs he pulled in were damp and did not burn well. He dried them by keeping them close to the fire. The second time he went to find more wood it was too dark to see, and the two branches he managed to pull back with him were very heavy which meant they were full of moisture. There was nothing more he could do. He hoped, however, that he would get some much needed rest.

NINETEEN

Unclean Forest

VILIE WOKE REFRESHED. He had slept through the night. No night noises to disturb him and no animals had come near his shelter. The fire was still smouldering when he woke. He carefully placed dry twigs atop the embers, and heated his tea water over the flames. While the tea was boiling he went to the stream to wash his face. The water had collected in a still pool. Vilie looked down at his reflection in the translucent pool, and was startled to see a young girl's face appear behind him. He let out a small cry and quickly turned round to see if he had been followed, but there was no one there.

Vilie stared and stared at his reflection but he did not see the girl again. Could he have deceived himself? He wondered. But, no – he had seen her very clearly for a half second before he reacted. And now he was quite sure she was not a human, but one of the many spirit dwellers of the forest. What a beautiful face it was. He could not recall the features of the girl's face, just the way she looked at him in the mirror made by the pool. A tranquil gaze through soft eyes that looked on him with a look he could not describe just yet. Was it pity? No, it was not that but something that could only be defined as sympathy. Ridiculous as that might sound, it was true. She had looked sympathetically at the man before disappearing from view.

Nothing further happened. Vilie fetched water and walked back to his shelter – his head full of thoughts. It was true then what the old people said of the unclean forest. There were others who made it their home. He tried to think of the rules of hospitality. If he took firewood or gathered herbs from the forest, he should acknowledge the owners. What was it his mother used to say when they had gathered herbs so many years ago? *Terhuomia peziemu.* Thanks be to the spirits. He knew what she meant by that. If he found an animal in his traps and brought it home, she would repeat that. *Terhuomia pezie.* It was her way of pronouncing a prayer of thanksgiving to the provider, to Ukepenuopfü.* All the Tenyimia† worshipped the deity they called Ukepenuopfü, the birth-spirit, the creator of all. Vilie wondered if he should pronounce his mother's words, but it felt a little silly when he could see no one around to address it to.

He turned his attention to the meal he was cooking.

---

* Ukepenuopfü: The creator deity worshipped in the old religion of the Tenyi people.

† Teynimia: largest linguistic group made of nine tribes speaking the same language, Tenyidie.

He looked for and found some of the *senyiega** that was a favourite of the *gwi*. He took some tender leaves of the tree ferns sprouting by the stream. It was good both for man and animal. It went into his pot and he added more salt to the broth. It was soon ready as the tender ferns did not need to be cooked long. Vilie took out a good portion, and kept the rest of the food aside for the evening. After eating he spent his afternoon gathering firewood for the night. He found dry wood on the edge of the forest. The dead wood within the forest never got enough sunshine to dry, so he took as much as he could of the dry wood he found on the outskirts of the forest. He would make sure he was well prepared for another night in the unclean forest. His plan was to travel in the morning. He felt safe here and a little more rest wouldn't hurt.

Vilie found wild ginseng and made a paste of it and smeared it on his ankles and wrists. He pulled out the root of one and smashed it with a rock. Then he put the ginseng into his tea mug and soaked it in hot water. After it had soaked, he drank down the mixture. Vilie had much faith in the restorative properties of the plant. Although it was touted as an aphrodisiac, he knew it also had healing properties which were not commonly known. Before it got really dark, he fell fast asleep. The fire had been piled up with enough wood to last the night. It was good wood as was to be expected from a forest like this.

---

* Senyiega: tree fern.

TWENTY

Forest Etiquette

VILIE COULD NOT MOVE. He was being chased by angry spirits that were about to catch up with him. But he was paralysed by cramps in his calves that prevented him from taking even one step further. The leader of the spirits was a hair-covered old man who was in a terrible rage. Cursing and spitting, he jumped on Vilie's back and began to pull out his hair. The pain made Vilie cry out. He saw that the other spirits were closing in on him and he was terrified of what horrific death they would visit upon him. Presently he woke with a start, and relief washed over him as he realised it was only a dream. The relief did not last for long. He could not move. What was wrong with him? His feet and legs would not budge. There was a heavy weight on his chest and Vilie thought it was part of his dream. But the weight was real enough. A dark, indistinguishable shape was sitting on top of him, and for the life of him all his efforts to dislodge it were in vain. He was screaming but the scream was stuck in his throat and his open mouth emitted no sound.

His throat felt as though it was stuffed with cotton wool. He formed the thought, "What do you want?" and flung it out at the shape atop him. He felt the spirit thing would detect his thought even if he had no power to speak to it. "What do you want from me? If I have done anything wrong, tell me so I can atone, for I have done nothing wrong deliberately." He sent out these thoughts like a prayer, more like a plea. There was no answer from the thing. The weight increased and Vilie feared his chest might be crushed under the terrible burden. He tried to move sideways and cause the thing to topple off, but it was stuck fast to him. He lay there inert and helpless, petrified by fear. What should he do next? Was this the end for him? Was he going to die here? No one would find him or dare to look for him in the unclean forest.

As these thoughts raced through his mind, causing him more grief and fear than he had ever known, Vilie suddenly remembered the seer's words. *Let your spirit be the bigger one. They are spirits, they will submit to the authority of the spirit that asserts itself.* It was a thought so bright and so clear it pierced his mind. His fear of the thing vanished with that thought. He gathered himself together. The thing now seemed to him so utterly detestable that he wanted to fling it off, and crush it under his feet. With a superhuman effort, Vilie summoned all his strength and pushed the thing off him. Stumbling to his feet he cried,

"Mine is the greater spirit! I will never submit to you!"

He had found his voice again and it echoed back to him.

He didn't even reach for his gun. Standing up straight he expanded his chest and shouted,

"Mine is the greater spirit! Depart from me!"

The thing lay where it had fallen as though wounded and defeated. It had no human shape. It was as misshapen as a hunchback but had no face to it. Vilie shouted at it to reveal itself and answer his questions but it seemed incapable of doing that.

"Then get out of here before I harm you!" Vilie shouted again and the thing grew smaller and smaller until it was just barely visible. Then it flung itself against a tree-trunk and stayed pasted to it, no bigger than a beetle. Vilie found he had no more interest in it.

The fire had died down so he went to stoke it with more wood. He fed it generously with the dry logs he had dragged in that afternoon. Now the forest was lit up from within and his little exercise had made his heart big. He wouldn't move out until it got lighter, he resolved. The forest was his as much as it was theirs. He had not caused any injury to any of them. Strengthened by these thoughts, he sat by the fire with his loaded gun. Eventually he fell asleep.

Bird calls heralded a new day. Vilie left the dying fire and went to the stream. He washed his face and stealthily crept to the pool and peered into it. There was nothing there. He stayed on, gazing at it. With the slightest of movements, she appeared and passed over the pool surface so he could see her for a longer time than yesterday. First, her face with the same kind look on it and then her hair, long, dark and flowing behind her and then she passed on and as Vilie continued to watch her, he saw that all that was to her was her face and her hair. There was no body attached to that beautiful face that floated past in the frosty morning air.

TWENTY-ONE

The Border Village

NOTHING COULD PERSUADE VILIE to linger in the unclean
forest after that final sight. He almost sped out of it.
Fortunately the exit he had chosen offered him a much
shorter route to the border village. He walked for an hour
on a path which abruptly ended at a precipice. To proceed
from there, he had to follow a steep path that took him to
the valley. It was much more difficult to descend than he
had thought. The path was narrow and jagged − the rock
face on the one side meant that a nasty fall awaited careless
travellers.

Vilie soon saw that he was not travelling alone. Ahead
of him were women returning from the Saturday market
bearing baskets holstered by a single strap around their
heads. The women were so used to the path that they walked
easily and went at a much faster pace than him. Vilie did not
want to be left behind so he tried to catch up with them.

When he drew closer he called out a greeting and they
replied without turning back to look at him.

"How long will it take to reach the village?" he asked.

The answer came from several of the women,

"Two hours."

It was better than he had hoped.

"Do you have a place to stay?" called out the last woman in the line.

When Vilie answered in the negative, she said he could be their guest. Her tone was welcoming. Her husband was the headman of the village and would be happy to host him, she added. Vilie expressed his gratitude and followed quietly behind them. After all the misadventures he had been having on the journey, including the scare he had had the night before, he was overcome with emotion by the show of human kindness. As he followed their footsteps, his eyes smarted slightly with the faintest suggestion of tears, which he hastily wiped away.

They reached the base of the slope, and the path widened so two or three people could walk alongside each other. Vilie and the woman, whose name was Subale, walked side-by-side and she explained that more and more of the young people were moving away to the towns like Dimapur or Peren. They found it too difficult to live as their parents did walking back and forth. The village had approached the government to construct a road, but the politicians told them the government did not have the money to make a road to the village.

"This is our home, do you understand? We cannot abandon it and try to live in another place. Our umbilical cords are buried here, and we would always be restless if we tried to settle elsewhere," Subale explained.

Vilie had heard that explanation before. His aunt's relative wanted to move to a warmer place, but she warned him that he would suffer from it later. She explained that the longing to return to the place where your umbilical cord was buried would become overwhelming as years went by, and that he would not be able to stay on in the new place.

"That is why we continue to live here," Subale went on. "But you must tell us what brings you here to our desolate village. You can tell your story to my husband when we have eaten and I will listen too."

The path widened slightly and they found themselves at the village. There were only a few houses. They were built on the slope above which the path ended. Vilie was surprised to see that the houses were built in such a way that they looked as though they were clinging to the slope, and there were steps cut into the rocky surface leading to each house. The path down to the river, which was their only water source, was another flight of steps or footholds carved into the rock. On the other side was the granite face of a mountain bereft of vegetation. So the border village was, in reality, a small settlement of determined people who had made their dwellings in an impossible place.

"How did you ever get building material down here?" asked an amazed Vilie.

"It wasn't easy," Subale admitted. "We insisted on using tin for our roofs but as for the rest, we improvised."

She narrated how they had cut wood from the forest above the valley and thrown logs down the hillside. Nails were easier to carry back from the markets but the tin was lowered down on long ropes. Vilie marvelled at the obstinacy of the people who called the isolated little village home. In wonderment, he followed Subale to the village headman's home.

TWENTY TWO

Fish for Dinner

"MY HUSBAND IS A FISHERMAN in addition to his job as headman," she said proudly.

The man they spoke of stood at the low doorway. With a broad smile he welcomed Vilie into their house. Subale's husband Kani, had cooked some fish which he had caught from the river earlier in the day. The smell of fresh bamboo shoots and green chilli permeated the kitchen and Vilie had to swallow hard because he was salivating.

The fish tasted incredibly good. Vilie relished every piece of the river fish and ate a healthy serving. They filled up his plate a second time and he did not turn down the generous helping.

"We live as our forefathers did. Fishing and drying the fish and selling it in the market so we can buy the things we can't make by ourselves. We use the brine pools for salt and we collect and sell the salt to buy tea and sugar at the market. More and more customers want fish from the river Barak, so there is really a high demand for it. Actually this is not the river Barak. It is a tributary though it looks very big indeed."

Kani was referring to the river above which the village lay. The roar of water could be heard all day from the village, though much reduced in volume.

"What about rice? Where do you grow that? Or do you just buy it?" Vilie asked curiously.

"Shall we show him our secret?" Kani asked Subale with a little wink.

"I'm sure we can trust him to keep it to himself," Subale responded, looking over at their guest.

Kani pointed to the window and indicated that Vilie should look out of it. Though it was getting dark, there was enough light outside for him to make out a very flat area of land with a row of rice fields west of the village. He could see paddy growing in neat lines there. Vilie was quite surprised.

"How come there is such a flat area there? Why don't you live over there instead of using it to grow rice? Wouldn't it be much easier to do that than climbing up rocks to get to your houses?"

"Ah, we could do that but we can't grow rice on these rocks where our houses stand. In any case, we have learnt from childhood to manoeuvre these rocks so we don't mind using the only piece of flat land we have for growing rice."

Vilie realised his questions had been ignorantly made. He quickly told them he hoped he hadn't been too impolite in asking so many questions.

"You are not the first who has asked us that," Kani laughed. Vilie liked this old couple who had taken him in without any hesitation. After a little pause, he began to tell them about his journey, and all the things that had happened to him on his way, including what he had seen in the unclean forest. He added that he was going to find the sleeping river. Now it was their turn to be astonished.

"Ordinary persons have no business to make the journey to our village. Before you came, only men with a definite purpose have come here. The river you speak of is beyond this one, but of course you know that. I will lead you there tomorrow," Kani offered.

Vilie was unwilling to accept the offer because he didn't want to bother anyone, so he tried to refuse help.

But Kani would not hear of Vilie trying to find the river alone.

"It is no bother. I insist on coming because it is a dangerous journey and you will not regret taking me along."

In the end Vilie agreed.

"The sleeping river is guarded by the widow women spirits. If you are protected they will not harm you, but if you are unprotected, you will be torn to pieces by them. You cannot go there ignorant of the rules."

Vilie asked what Kani meant by protection. He wanted to know if it resembled anything like the spirit challenge he had made to the spirit in the unclean forest. Kani pushed his shirt sleeve up, and showed Vilie a scar that ran all along his arm and ended near his wrist. A chunk of flesh had been taken out from the arm. It was an old wound that had healed, but the skin over it was stretched so thin, it looked membrane like.

"I was foolish enough to go out unprotected and paid for it with my arm," Kani began. "Remember when we are out at the sleeping river, there can be no room for fear. If you harbour fear, you are a dead man. If you came here after committing something terrible, like a murder or sending a man to his death by a false testimony, your spirit will not be able to outwrestle their spirits. Any evil action of yours will weigh on your conscience, and make you vulnerable to their onslaught. It is an attack, there's nothing gentle about it. So your protection is your own good heart and your clear conscience. Harbour no evil against any man when you are going on this trip."

TWENTY-THREE

The Sleeping River

THE NEXT MORNING THE TWO MEN readied themselves for their journey. Subale was up before them, and had prepared food that would provide much needed nutrition and energy: cooked rice and fish packed in plantain leaves. In a small bag she had packed puffed rice, so they would have some food reserves if their trip took longer than a day.

Kani carried his spear and his newly sharpened *dao* swung from its holder which he had strapped behind his back. He also had his bag slung on his shoulder with the food packets. Kani was about 72 but he looked much older. Deep lines on his face made him look like one of the rock carvings Vilie had seen outside his village. He was a small, wiry man who easily walked barefoot on his calloused soles. The treacherous rocky steps were no problem for him as he had manoeuvred them countless times from childhood. But he kept a slow pace so that Vilie would not stumble in trying to keep up with him. When they reached the end of the steps, they got to a plain ridge along which they walked for a long time. They arrived at a stream where they drank water and rested for some time.

"Some men have returned without ever catching the river," Kani stated, "but surely you have heard of that."

"No I haven't," Vilie responded. "There wasn't much I could learn about the river by way of information. The seer was quite cryptic and I had to try and interpret what he said as best as I could."

"There are men who have lost their lives trying to catch the river," Kani said in a lowered, almost imperceptible voice.

"I am not surprised by that. Did they drown or did they fall prey to fever?"

Kani scanned the horizon before he turned to Vilie.

"They came without knowledge, and that itself is enough to kill a man. They sought the stones they could use as charms to possess wealth. But that is not what the sleeping river is for. Certainly, if you catch it while it is sleeping, you can take out a stone from the river and use it to grant you blessings of wealth and cattle but there is more to it than that."

Vilie was intrigued by what Kani was saying.

"More to it? You mean it is wrong to seek the stones that bring wealth?"

"What joy will wealth afford you when you do not know the secret of living with peace and faith in your fellow men? It is not wrong to have wealth but your relationship to your wealth defines everything else. If you are grasping at wealth, you are going to lose something that wealth cannot buy for you. You will lose knowledge of the spiritual. And you will lose the power it offers you. That is true power; that is the only power to aspire to because it gives you power over both the world of the senses and the world of the spirit."

Vilie listened closely. He felt that he had come very far from the man who had left his forest home to go on a quest for the sleeping river. The past few days had taught him much and he paused to consider the whole adventure. Was it worth it to have undergone near-lynching by the men of Dichu village? Or the spirit encounter in the unclean forest where he was almost crushed to death? Not to speak of the weretiger who would have killed him if he had not used his owner's name to send him away. But he also thought of the woman at the forest of nettles who had been kind to him, and now he had met these people of the border village who were going out of their way to help a stranger.

He wanted to find the sleeping river. He wanted to catch it while it slept and wrest a river-heart-stone from the waters and take it back home with him. But most of all, he wanted the spiritual knowledge that the sleeping river would give him if they found it. Both for his own sake and for Kani's sake, he wanted now more than ever to find the river.

They ate the food they had carried with them and resumed their journey. By Kani's estimation they would reach the banks of the river in two hours, just before nightfall. Then they would have to proceed without talking to each other, using only the slightest of hand gestures to communicate, and that too only if it was absolutely necessary. It was not enough that they find the river. They would have to wait until it fell asleep and no one could tell how long that would be.

As they kept walking, the vegetation changed; it became more lush and green. Back at the border village, Vilie had seen the plants stubbornly pushing their way out through the rocks and struggling to stay alive, looking skeletal and undernourished. But here the ferns effortlessly grew tall and lush, spreading themselves out. Plantain trees dotting the landscape were top-heavy with fruit, but these were wild bananas and not fit for human consumption. Birds were in abundance, flying overhead or calling from treetops where they were feeding on the overripe fruit.

Suddenly Kani held up his hand, signalling Vilie to stop talking. Vilie stopped instantly in his tracks and peered in the direction Kani was pointing to. But Vilie saw nothing. Kani looked at him and mouthed the words, "very close, very close." They then proceeded cautiously, avoiding dead leaves that would crackle under their feet, and give their presence away. After a good two hours of walking in this manner, Kani raised his hand again and signalled Vilie to stop.

"The river," he mouthed and he dropped down to his knees. Again Vilie saw nothing but he heard the faint

sound of water over rocks up ahead. They had reached the
sleeping river at last! A great sense of excitement overcame
him and he sank to his knees – staying there for some time.
Kani signalled that they would stay put, and they arranged
themselves more comfortably to prepare for the long wait.

TWENTY-FOUR

Stone and Flood

AS SOON AS THEY ENTERED the territory of the sleeping river, all birdsong ceased. In fact, the silence was deafening. Not a leaf stirred, and there was not the faintest of insect cheeping to break the silence. No human sound polluted the forest where the river lay. The men breathed as gently as they could, feeling that the very breaths they exhaled were an affront to the utter purity of the place. There was so little suggestion of the flesh here.

Vilie tried to remember what the seer had said. He had spoken in very vague terms about patience and courage. Wait and wait until you are ready, he had said. Wait until you are more than ready, to be half ready is not enough. He was more than willing to wait and learn. He was so wary of making a wrong move. They crouched and waited until the muscles in their ankles were protesting. To change positions took a lot of time and effort as they did not want to make any sound. At the same time, Vilie did not want to risk getting cramps in his legs when the time came to catch the river. So he carefully slid out his legs and lay on the ground, his head turned toward the direction in which the water sounds came. Kani signalled that they would proceed onward and closer to the river. Vilie imitated Kani's every movement. The wiry little fisherman crept on the ground and moved forward by pressing with his palms downward, pulling his body forward. They both did this very slowly. Eventually they came to a point where the river grew louder, with ever deeper tones.

Vilie's ears resounded with the cascade of a mighty waterfall and the swift and powerful rush of water over the protruding rocks. The river must be very big, Vilie thought to himself. As they moved on and dragged themselves closer and closer to the sounds, the noise of the cataract receded and after a while, all they could hear was the tinkling of water as though from a streamlet. Vilie marvelled at this but Kani did not seem to find anything unusual about it. He restrained himself from asking what it meant, and followed the fisherman further on. They were climbing upward now, and the sounds of a river upstream came clearly to them. Sometimes Vilie thought he heard fish leaping, but could not be quite sure. He stopped to look up at the river. There was a hazy blue fog that covered everything from view, and he never saw anything beyond the river fog. Surprisingly they saw no birds. Not even the big birds that would be feeding on fish, like the kingfisher or hawks which frequented these hills. The sound of fish leaping came again and Vilie stopped to watch but as before, he saw nothing.

Finally Kani halted as the path eased off onto a plain stretch. Everything was still. No river or fish sounds. Not even the hint of a breeze. It was rapidly getting dark, and they could only see the shadowy outlines of trees and the big rocks on the river's edge. Vilie raised his head and saw a smooth body of water lying perfectly still. It was the sleeping river at last. Very excited at finally finding it, Vilie thought it was time to go down into the river but Kani held up his hand to indicate that he should not move.

They stayed like that for an infinitely long period of time. Then they saw them, the spirit widow-women who guarded the river. They carried baskets on their backs and walked into the fog and down to the river. They looked as though they were fetching water but their water pots stayed in their baskets. After the strange ritual, they retreated and went up the bank. They chanted as they walked back - a haunting little chant that Vilie thought he had heard before. Not in his waking moments, but in dreams and shadow moments between waking and dreaming. It was the saddest sound he had ever heard. The widow-women continued climbing the path above the river, and their chanting followed them upward until it receded and the men could no longer see them. In the half-light it was difficult to make out whether they were human or not, but Vilie was quite sure that there could be nothing human about the basket-carrying, black-clad figures retreating up the hillside. There was something so forbidding about them; both in the chanting that so strongly resembled funeral chants and in the stern way they held themselves as they walked in file back to wherever they had their bleak lodgings.

Vilie remembered what Subale had said about the very brief interval between the time that the widow-women disappeared behind the hills, and the river stopped flowing and went to sleep. If he made his heart big he could catch the river at that time, but if he faltered, it might be months before the opportunity came to him again. Perhaps even years. Vilie impatiently looked over at Kani. The fisherman raised his hand and mouthed, "Now!" Without a second's hesitation, Vilie ran to the edge and plunged into the unmoving river. The water was incredibly cold. Undeterred, he reached down and grabbed a stone from the middle of the river. It was stuck fast to the floor and Vilie felt his fingers stiffening from the cold. He would not let go and find another one. Instead he gave it a mighty tug and the stone came away. Abruptly the waters flowed again, in a furious spate this time flooding over him and pushing him under just as it had happened in his dream.

TWENTY-FIVE

"The River is a Spirit!"

VILIE WAS FLUNG BACK like a bit of driftwood by the inrushing waters. His mouth and nostrils filled up with water as he felt himself being sucked down by the treacherous undercurrent. The river was almost human as it pushed him down and under, down and under, and the water rushed at him as though it would strangle him. He was shocked at the violence of the river. "I'm going to get out of this alive!" he swore as he fought back. At first he flailed his arms helplessly as he had in his nightmare-dreams of the river. But this was terrifyingly real. He would not wake up and cry with relief that it was only a dream. This was as real as real could be. Then he stopped struggling and concentrated instead on the spirit words he had learnt: "Sky is my father, Earth is my mother, stand aside death! Kepenuopfü fights for me, today is my day! I claim the wealth of the river because mine is the greater spirit. To him who has the greater spirit belongs the stone!"

How long he kept fighting the river Vilie did not know,

but it seemed like an eternity before he was released and the waters retreated and he could step out of it unharmed, clutching the heart-stone. Kani was standing anxiously by the edge and pulled him out swiftly as he emerged from the river.

"Come on, we have to run back before the widow-women come after us!"

It was the first time Kani had spoken all afternoon and the urgency in his voice was very real. Vilie heard a shriek and looked upward at its source, and saw black figures descending toward them. The widow-women were running down the hill, waving thin spears and shouting curses on the two men.

"Run!" cried Kani.

But Vilie needed no urging. He clambered after Kani disregarding the small stones that cut his feet and the thorns that made his feet bleed. He ran for his life as the widow-women chased them wildly. While the widow-women were still on the far bank of the river, the men got out of the river area. The water had completely receded, and they fled for their lives. Even as they sped on, they could hear sounds of hissing and grunting behind them. Neither dared to look back. They ran as swiftly as they could, Vilie clutching the stone to him and Kani with his twisted arm in front of him, leaping goat-like over the high rocks in his way. They heard different sounds behind them: first, it was the cackling of old, old women, the sound of malicious victory. That was followed by laughter, the gurgling laughter of babies and children, innocent and enticing, urging them to look back. As the men carried on running, the laughter turned to high pitched shrieks as the widow-women spirits tried to threaten and frighten the two men.

When they reached the outer path which marked the boundary between the sleeping river and the border village, Kani shouted at the widow women, "Back! Back now or the worse for you!" The shrieks stopped instantly and they withdrew. But they wailed as they went, their ghoulish wailing filling the air and polluting it.

"*Kepenuopfü zanu tsie la mha talie!*"* shouted Kani and the evil sounds stopped abruptly.

The widow-women sank down to the ground defeated. The two men did not stop to see if they resumed their original shapes or not. They headed for the village not exchanging a word, but each thinking to himself the thoughts that strengthened his spirit.

---

* Kepenuopfü zanu tsie la mha talie: In the name of the creator-deity retreat at once.

Genna Day

SUBALE WAS WAITING AT THE DOOR as they climbed up the steps. She held the door open to let them in, and then shut it quickly and loudly once the men were safely inside. She had no welcoming smile for them. But that was only because she was all too familiar with the events of the night and levity was far from every mind. Silently she looked at each man and shook her head, to show she marvelled at their return. She gave them warm water to wash themselves and she knelt to help her husband wash his feet. Then she served them food by the fire.

Vilie was trembling as he sat down to warm himself. He thought it was from the cold but the warmth of the fire did nothing to ease his trembling. Kani fetched a blanket and draped it over him.

"This is what comes after a spirit encounter. The flesh trembles even while the spirit is triumphant, because the flesh cannot understand that you have won the battle, and it struggles with its own memories of fear."

Vilie gratefully wrapped the blanket around himself. He was more than grateful for Kani's sacrifice in accompanying him to the sleeping river. He had saved them both. Those terrible widow-women, they were much more frightening than the incident in the river. They were certainly not human though their name suggested some links with humans in the past. How they had relentlessly chased them as though hungry to draw blood. They probably were. Vilie shivered involuntarily.

"Was it one of the widow-women who tore the flesh from your arm?" he had to ask.

"It certainly was. Don't underestimate their unbelievable strength. They have the tendons of bulls. I had no option but to let her tear half my arm off in order to save my life. Had I not done that I would have surely died. That was the most horrible sight I have ever seen. She took my torn ligaments and stuffed them down her mouth, my blood dribbling down the sides of her mouth as she feasted on my flesh.I had stopped running – the pain was so intense. But when I saw she was hungry for more, I dashed out of there ignoring the searing pain. Having gone through that ordeal, I could not possibly let you go there alone."

Vilie was horrified by Kani's account. He did not doubt for a second that it was true. Now he had to ask all the questions that had been plaguing him.

"Why did you take me? Wouldn't it have been better to warn me and let me go back?"

"Hmm, why did I take you? Difficult question," Kani

began and rubbed the back of his head. "Maybe because you are different from the others who have come here before you. Because your spirit is large-hearted and teachable, and because I sensed you would be more amenable to spirit things than the others were. Perhaps there is a deeper reason why you felt so drawn to seek the heart-stone."

"The river is a spirit too, isn't it?" Vilie questioned. "It receded when I fought it with the words I was taught by the seer. It acceded to my authority. And it diminished in power when I asserted my identity."

"Indeed the river is a spirit. Spirit responds to spirit. Your gun is useless against the things of the spirit for these are not flesh and blood."

There was a long pause after Kani said this. Then Vilie turned round to face him.

"Thank you." There were tears in his eyes.

The fisherman smiled slightly.

"Thank yourself for your faith. You couldn't have made it without that."

When they were done eating they retired to their beds. Thankfully sleep came instantly, a restful deep sleep undisturbed by nightmares or waking dreams. Vilie slept until the sun's rays stole into the room through little cracks in the walls and grew longer and brighter.

He lay for a bit more, listening to his hosts moving around.

"You should tell him it is a *genna-day*,* and it is good for him to rest on a *genna-day*."

"They probably don't do this anymore where he comes from but he is a wise one. I'm sure he will understand it is dangerous to travel on a *genna-day*."

Vilie got out of bed quickly and joined them.

"Hope you don't mind me asking – what was that about today being a *genna-day*?"

"Every time a person catches the sleeping river, we who live here observe a *genna-day*, a no-work day. The villagers here will not do any work in their fields today. They will not go fishing or go to look at their traps. It is a day of thanksgiving for delivered lives. You would do well not to travel on a *genna-day* especially since it is being observed for you."

"Nothing would persuade me to violate such a wonderful custom, especially if it is being observed on my account. I can rest a whole day. It will do me good," Vilie replied.

He welcomed the wisdom of resting to recover his strength before he journeyed back.

---

* Genna-day: a no-work day strictly observed by the village for religious reasons. Those who violate it are penalised.

TWENTY-SEVEN

The Way Back

THE REST DAY DID HIM GOOD. Kani fetched a bottle of dark oil and massaged it into his legs and ankles saying it would help the soreness go away. At first the oil burnt him and Vilie wondered if it would really do him any good. Then the burning eased and it felt relaxing and soothing all at once. Vilie lay back and enjoyed the oil penetrating his skin and opening up his pores.

The next day Subale packed a lot of food for him. Besides cooked rice and fish, she had packed dried fish and uncooked rice so he would have food for the rest of his journey. The wife and husband hovered around him like a pair of hens. It both amused and touched Vilie. They seemed to want to impart all of their wisdom to him before he left.

"You know that you are in even more danger now because you possess the heart-stone. There are people who would give their lives to possess that stone. Even the spirit creatures envy you now that you have the heart-stone, and they will try to take it from you either by force or deceit. Be very careful. Tell no one you have it."

"I am not even sure I know what its full powers are," Vilie answered.

"It is a charm that grants wealth if you ask if for wealth. It grants abundant cattle, or prowess in war. It can also grant success with women if you want that. The reason why so many want it is because it grants success in battle. Can you imagine how unequal the fight would be if one party had the heart-stone with them?"

"Fortunately, it is only a human who can enter the sleeping river to catch the river," Subale spoke up, "Spirits cannot do that. They cannot touch water, certainly not the water of the sleeping river because that is a spirit too."

"Tell him more about that," Kani urged his wife.

"Yes, yes. My father told me it would cause spirit to ignite with spirit if that happened. That is why the widow-women cannot cross over to our village when the sleeping river is in full spate."

"Ah the strange, strange ways of the spirit world," Kani said with a smile.

"And the spirits want the stone because it has the power to turn the hearts of others to the owner. That is why spirits are so interested in the heart-stone," Subale concluded.

Vilie's mind was confused with all the information he had received about the stone. He hoped he would remember it all. It was mid-morning by the time he finished eating the meal Subale had set before them.

"I must be on my way," he said. "If I am to find shelter other than the unclean forest, I really should go now."

"One last word of advice," Kani began again, "Do not hesitate to use the name when you are desperate. The name is all powerful. If you use the name, you can destroy the power of any evil spirit attacking you."

"I will surely remember that," Vilie replied.

Subale came to stand beside him as though she wanted to say something too. Vilie finished tying the knot on his bag and looked up at her.

"Spirits use guile. They will appear to be good and beautiful so long as they can deceive you with appearances. Trust no one, not even yourself. Be alert all the time."

Vilie thanked them profusely and got up to go, his bag on his shoulder, his gun slung over his left arm. His hosts did not attempt to delay him further. They parted and he walked at his usual quick pace, trying to get up the rocky ledge that was the entrance to the border village, before the afternoon was spent. It was hard going but he was happy to be on his way back with the heart-stone. It had made his journey worthwhile. He still felt he did not know the full worth of the mysterious stone, but he had an inkling how precious it must be if men would risk life and limb to find it. And the spirits wanted it too, and they would take it by guile or by force. Perhaps the journey back might prove to be more difficult than the journey he had made to the river. Yet he felt prepared in a way. *Use the name*, Kani had advised. He had heard Kani use the name when they were running from the widow-women. He had used the name himself when he stood in the river and fought it. And it had worked.

TWENTY-EIGHT

Circumventions

VILIE FOUND HIMSELF BACK ON THE ROCK FACE with the sharp little footholds carved into the rock. He started climbing them carefully, stopping to rest briefly and continuing again. When he reached the top, he slowed a bit and looked down. It felt like a lifetime since he had gone down those steps and experienced all that he had from then on. From this vantage point, the border village was hidden from view. No one would suspect that there was a settlement there. Oddly enough, this was a comforting thought. He never wanted anything bad to happen to the people who lived there. Their fortress-like home, in spite of its hardships, would protect them from the greed of man.

The winds were very rough on the rock face, and he felt vulnerable standing on the edge as he was. So he moved back and retraced his steps the way he had come. Vilie soon reached the place where he had met Subale and the other women from the border village. That had been on a Saturday, and the women had been returning from the

Saturday market. He had spent three days in the border village. If he walked fast, he might come to the Tuesday market and be able to find shelter for the night in a village. He did not wish to spend the night in the forest or in a lonely field. He felt he had not recuperated sufficiently from the spirit encounters of the past days, and had no inclination to take on any more.

Ahead of him were outlines of mountains in the distant horizon. But the fields stretched to the foot of the mountains and Vilie knew that if there were fields, there would be villages not too far from the fields. If he could walk that far, he would be safe for the night. He walked on, reluctant to stop for a break and a meal. He wanted to cover as much distance as he could and be clear of the unclean forest area while it was still light. This time he decided to circumvent the unclean forest and take a route that went around it. Perhaps he was being unnecessarily cautious, but he wanted to be as safe as possible. He managed to put some distance between himself and the forest, but not so much as to miss the Tuesday market and the prospect of finding a host for the night. From where he stood he could see the tall trees of *Rarhuria*. Even from this distance, he saw that the unclean forest was darker than the rest of the other forest areas around it. He wondered whether it was due to foliage, or whether there were other reasons. When he looked at it attentively, the unclean forest seemed to be moving, a slow heaving forward and backward. Vilie averted his eyes and rubbed them hard. He didn't care to know anything about the unclean forest anymore.

The path that Vilie used was an old one still frequented by villagers who knew the crossings that led to different villages. Along the way, he saw many fig trees. The Zeliangs did not like to cut down the fig tree. They called it their brother-tree because one of their folk tales told them of a fig tree that had helped to hide a man of their tribe, and saved him from being killed by spirits. Fruit hung heavily from the branches. Most were not ready, but there were at least two or three that were ripe and bursting. Vilie resisted the temptation to stop and pick fruit and carried on walking. When he felt he was at a safe enough distance from the unclean forest, he slowed down and veered off the path to rest in a small clearing.

The fish meal Subale had packed in two sets of leaves was still fragrant. Barak river fish - it had no scales and she had used country ginger and green chilli to spice it. The special garnish allowed the fish flavour to come out without overpowering it. It tasted like roasted fish - the way the fishermen prepared it. They stuffed a fresh catch inside a large bamboo and roasted it slowly over coals. This made the fish retain all of its texture and subtle taste. Fishermen in these parts never carried pots, but simply cut down arm-length sections of bamboo and stuffed their catch inside the bamboo, covered the open end with herbs and slowly cooked the fish over glowing coals.

Replenished, Vilie quickly disposed of the leaves and

packed his things to continue the journey. Already ants were marching in a line to the leaves. He tossed a few grains of rice at them and laughed as they scattered to pick them up – though the rice grains were much larger than the ants themselves.

TWENTY-NINE

Tuesday Market

AT THE NEXT CURVE IN THE BEND the path widened, and then it met with the big countryside road. Vilie heard the sound of many voices coming from a short distance away. It was the Tuesday market. Somehow he had stumbled upon it on his circuitous route. He had no idea what villages might be congregated at this Tuesday market but he was sure he would meet some people who spoke his language. He walked faster. Yet the faster he walked the further the market seemed to be and at one point, he wondered whether his ears were deceiving him. The truth was that he was walking in the plains where sound carried for long distances, and was often amplified by the flatness of the terrain.

He soon came to the field where the market had been set up. A huge, sprawling, colour–drenched market where traders had stalls selling every imaginable item. Vegetable growers were selling potatoes, cauliflower, tomatoes, eggplants, okra and long beans in carefully stacked heaps. Women buyers were flocking to these stalls because it was now an hour to closing time, and the sellers had brought the prices down. In the other stalls, dark-skinned men from the plains sold children's toys, and little whistles and toy trumpets which they occasionally blew, adding to the clamour of the market. Beside the toy seller, the ice cream man's ices were melting and stray dogs licked at the sweet fluids on the ground. The candyfloss man was happily drinking tea at another stall, having sold all his cotton candy.

Women's dresses and shoes, sunglasses, and shiny, coloured plastic handbags hung in the next stall. Two girls stood looking at the women's dresses. They were very beautiful and Vilie looked twice in their direction. Slender-limbed and long-haired, they reminded him of the face he had seen in the unclean forest. He didn't want to look a third time as that would have been rude, so he moved on.

Umbrellas, rain boots, carpentry tools and men's underwear were all being sold under one roof in another stall. And so it went on, stall after stall and people flowed in and out of the market, stopping here and then there, trying to pick up a good bargain before the sellers decided they had had enough and packed their goods away. If they did that, there was no persuading them to sell their wares. A very persistent buyer could get a seller to unpack and sell him something he really wanted, but that did not happen often.

These last few minutes before closing time were crucial. Experienced buyers knew how to make a good bargain and the last hour saw much desperate haggling. These buyers were the ones who followed the market from one market day to another. They knew exactly when the shops would open, and what goods would be sold on which day. They could reel off the names of the items on their fingertips, and were looked up to as being experts. They had their uses, for people liked to consult them on what were the best prices to pay for a certain item. These were the ones Vilie came upon when he reached the market – the lingerers; the ones who stayed until the very end and gazed longingly after the dusty streets along which the sellers were departing with their wares.

Vilie watched these men and women, wondering who he should strike up a conversation with. An old man stood watching them too. Vilie felt him shift his glance, and he looked enquiringly at the old man.

He had an amused smile on his face. Before Vilie could speak he said,

"Funny lot, aren't they? One would think they go home every market day having bought all the goods at the market. Quite amazing, the way they come back for more every time."

"They certainly have a way about them," Vilie said lightly.

The old man turned his gaze away from the buyers and looked intently at Vilie.

"You are not from these parts. I can see that straightaway. What are you doing here at such a time?"

"You're right, I am not from around here. I am travelling through but am late and need to find a place to spend the night."

The old man smiled at him.

"If you don't mind spending the night in an old man's humble and not too clean lodgings, you are welcome to be my guest."

Vilie did not know how to reply to this offer which had come his way so unexpectedly. He looked closely at the old man but there was only friendliness and sincerity in that face.

"I don't want to be a scaremonger, but it's not good to linger behind when a market is done. There are other beings that come to mingle with the market folk and they stay on after the sellers and buyers have left. You don't want to be around then – alone with them. I'd be happy to share my home with you for the night."

Vilie accepted gratefully and followed the old man home. In the traditional way, he addressed him as Anie, paternal uncle. The house was old and badly in need of repair, but it had a door which closed and bamboo walls that were still standing.

"I did warn you," the old man laughed as he led Vilie into the interior of his house.

It was a single room divided by a thin curtain. The first part of the room was obviously his bedroom. They went into the kitchen area and Vilie laid his gun and bag down.

"Markets are marvellous things my son, but many men

have been deceived at markets. Therefore I go there and try to save as many as I can. Sometimes, like today, there were only known people so that made my job lighter."

"What do you mean by that? Are you talking about the sellers cheating the buyers?"

"Ah no, nothing as straightforward as that. A flurry of human activity such as the market always attracts the river spirits. They are beautiful female spirits. You might even have seen them at some time never suspecting they are spirits. They appear as beautiful young girls and mingle with the market people. Sometimes they try on bangles and anklets and the seller remembers them. He always remembers them because he has never seen such beautiful and delicate ankles before that he simply wants to gift all his anklets to them. That is all right but the really dangerous thing is that they come to the markets to look for bridegrooms – young men that they can marry and make wealthy. But these men always die young. That is how it is with the river-spirits and the markets where they seek their prey."

Vilie instantly thought of the two beautiful girls he had seen by the women's clothing stall. Could they have been river-spirits? But they had looked so real. And they were extremely beautiful. He had felt like looking at them all evening.

"Ah well, you must get some rest now. If I start talking there will be no end to it."

Vilie thanked his host and went to bed, thankful that a

long fireside conversation was not expected of him. He was quite tired from his long excursion.

THIRTY

The Village of the Kirhupfümia

VILIE WOKE REFRESHED and looked for his host to thank him. The old man was not anywhere around. Just as a feeling of foreboding was coming upon him, he heard footsteps and a low laugh.

"Don't worry, I am quite real." His host laughed as he brought in a bundle of freshly plucked herbs from outside.

"Here is our morning meal," he said cheerily as he put it on a small wooden table and teased the fire.

Vilie got up and washed his face. He helped separate the leaves and tender stalks and toss them into the pot. The old man had boiled dried meat and salt and dried chilli. The chilli was so pungent it made Vilie cough.

"The only cure for that is to lick up some salt," said his host as he quickly passed Vilie the salt container. Vilie took a bit of salt and put it on his tongue and the coughing receded.

"Anie, that is remarkable!" he said.

"It's the saltiness of salt that counteracts the effect of chilli and neutralises it," the old man stated.

As they finished their modest meal, the old man looked directly at Vilie and said:

"My son, I know that you are carrying a heavy secret. You do not have to fear me because I am too old to keep secrets. My life is an open book to all who pass by. But you, you have something in your possession that many other men will want. They will not want to share it with you but they will seek to steal it from you. Likewise, the spirits will come after you to steal it. So guard it well and guard your own heart too. Do not be deceived and do not let your heart deceive you either."

"What do you mean by that, Anie?" Vilie asked.

"Others will seek to deceive you. It may come as a seduction of your senses, it may come as a good thing that you cannot find any fault with, and when that happens your own heart will deceive you. Then you will be in danger of losing the heart-stone. Yes I know you have the heart-stone with you."

"Did you go through my bag when I was asleep?" Vilie asked, surprised that the old man knew his secret.

"No, but I am old enough to tell when a man is carrying the heart-stone. There is something that sets him apart from all other men. You did not go after the beautiful river-spirits in the market yesterday as any other fool would have done. You sought neither to purchase nor possess the trinkets of the market. There was an otherness about you that I saw when I first spoke to you. Yet I took care not to seem too interested in you in case you suspected I was after your heart-stone. You have found that which is of ultimate worth and you should guard it with your life."

Vilie was convinced more than ever of the preciousness of the heart-stone, and he felt for it in his bag. Then he took it out and held it in his cupped palm. The stone was more oval than round. They both looked at it closely. The light from the fire shone on it and gave it a translucent glow, a purplish hue that caught sparks of light and glimmered. They both gasped at the beauty of the stone. Vilie placed it on the ground away from the fire. He placed it below the window where the natural light would fall on it directly. When he did that, the stone lost its purple glow and lay there looking like any ordinary stone. There were markings down the side of the stone, deep grooves that made it look ugly and worthless.

"Ah, so that is how it saves itself from an unbeliever," said the old man knowingly.

"What do you mean, Anie?" Vilie asked.

"What we saw first was its real self. But when you placed it in natural light, it looked totally unattractive. That is how an unbeliever would see it, and never see any value in it and simply pass by it."

"But a spirit is a believer and would still recognise it even if it looked ugly and worthless, wouldn't it?"

Vilie had answered his own question. He replaced the stone in his bag and prepared to go. He thanked his host and set off once more, promising to be careful. The old man's parting words echoed in his head, *take the road left, every time you come to a crossroads, always take the road that points left.* Vilie wondered what that meant but decided he would go ahead and find out for himself. He had made a good start today, and he saw the valley spreading before him, the yellowing fields looking ready for an early harvest. From this point, he had a much better view of the area before him and he proceeded confidently. He was headed for the mountain range beyond the fields, the same mountains he had seen the night before. If he could reach the foot of the mountains by evening, there would surely be a village nearby to shelter in. He thought he could see the tin roofs of houses glinting in the sun.

When he had crossed all the fields, he saw there was indeed a village not far from the last of the fields. It looked like the same village he had seen from afar with its roofs of tin. There were some houses lying close together and a few cows grazing. Vilie decided to survey the village a bit before he approached it. So he climbed the hill directly facing the village and looked down from that vantage point. He had a good view of everything that was going on. There were women working everywhere, but not a single man to be seen anywhere. The women were weaving or herding cows or husking grain. He thought the menfolk were out hunting or at some ceremonial occasion, at the same time, he could not help reflecting on the strangeness of a village where the men were completely missing. Nonetheless he felt safe to approach them for shelter and went down the path to the village.

It took him half the day to walk the whole length of the fields. Many of the villages had fields adjoining each other so when he had finished crossing a range of fields, he came upon another and yet another. He did not stop to eat. He wanted to reach the village as soon as possible.

Dogs barked at his approach and the women quickly stopped what they were doing and came towards him. He looked at their faces and saw that they appeared undisguisedly hostile. A tall woman with long hair stood with her hands on her hips, watching him with her lips drawn back to reveal her teeth. She looked like a dog about to attack. Vilie thought about making a quick retreat. All of a sudden, a younger woman moved forward, pushed the tall woman aside and pulled him by the sleeve.

"You shall be my guest for I have cooked meat tonight and have no one to share it with."

Vilie had no time to reconsider the proposal. The tall woman snarled and tried to grab Vilie's bag. But the younger woman was too quick for her. She stepped between the two of them and shielded Vilie, at the same time pushing the tall one away. At least the younger woman looked pleasant and certainly more welcoming than the older woman, so Vilie let her lead him to her home.

THIRTY-ONE

Love and Life

WHEN THEY ENTERED THE HOUSE, he felt a cold chill run down his spine. These were not ordinary women. His heart beat faster and he felt fear creep in at the thought. But he took hold of himself and looked around him. The interior of her house looked no different from that of any other house in a village. At the entrance hung the rain-shields made of plantain leaves that people used when it rained. Next to the rain-shields she had hung up a number of implements for field work, long-handled spades and hoes, and a scythe. Above the fire were baskets of dried herbs and fermented soya beans wrapped in plantain leaves. On the walls of the kitchen were different herbs hung out to dry. The kitchen was dark and smoke-filled and an earthen pot simmered over the fire.

"We shall eat meat tonight, did I not say so? You certainly look as though you could do with a good meat dinner."

Her name was Ate and the tall woman she had pushed away was her sister Zote. She called him by his name and

Vilie felt confused as he was sure he had not had a chance to introduce himself properly. Ate served him a plate of steaming rice topped with pieces of meat.

"Eat before the light goes, and then you may tell me your story."

Vilie's nostrils caught the aromatic whiff of meat but he had lost all appetite.

"First, you must tell me where I am. Where is your husband my dear hostess? What clan is this whose hospitality I am about to partake of?"

"Do not worry, there is nothing poisonous in the food. The meat is beef that I got someone to buy at the market. My husband will not come because I have no husband. I live alone as do the other women in the village. Eat and we will talk." She smiled pleasantly at him and he felt he was being impolite to question her in that manner when she had gone out of her way to be kind to him. So he thanked her and ate the food. It tasted very good as he had not eaten all day. The meat was tender and spiced with garlic and some ginger. She set down a mug of water beside his plate and he felt thirsty as soon as he saw the water.

"Won't you eat?" he asked her.

"I will," she said and she took out food for herself and ate with him. As they ate Vilie stole glances at her but she looked completely ordinary. She had a pleasing face, with the rosy cheeks of the Tenyi women who lived in the hills. She had kind eyes and Vilie wondered what was it about her that made him feel uneasy. He had his bag close to his foot though it was on the floor, and he ate with one eye always on the woman, watching her every move. When the meal was over, she poured him a mug of red tea and sat down by the fire.

"If I had not pulled your arm and taken you home, my sister would have killed you or worse."

"You mean the tall one? Is she your sister?"

"Yes."

"Who are you? What village is this I have come to?"

"This is the village of Kirhupfümia.* You have doubtless heard of us when you lived in your village. But do not worry for you are safe so long as you are with me in my house or under my protection. The others cannot harm you when you are with me."

Vilie could not help the shudder that went through him at her news. Kirhupfümia. They were the most feared persons in the mountains and here he was about to spend the night in their village. In a flash, he remembered what he had heard of them back in his ancestral village. He recalled the story of an old woman from the upper clan, feared by everyone and referred to as Kirhupfümia. People came to her with the first of their harvests, be it vegetables or fruit or grain and even eggs, chickens and bigger animals. Parents warned their children never to neglect to greet the old woman. She was said to have enormous evil powers.

---

* Kirhupfiimia: certain females believed to have poisonous powers and greatly feared.

Vilie also remembered Subale's parting words to him, *Spirits use guile. They will appear to be good and beautiful so long as they can deceive you with appearances. Trust no one, not even yourself.* Could he trust his hostess? She looked no more than a girl yet she had saved him from her sister. Did she do that so she could steal the stone herself? The woman who called herself Ate looked over at him.

"Kirhupfümia are outcasts in every village they are born into. Therefore we have come here and we live by ourselves where we have nothing to fear from each other and from others. And the villages we fled from have nothing to fear from us now. We never chose to be the way we are. It is the destiny life chose to give us.

"Back in our ancestral village a woman was very cruel to my sister. She would spit in our direction every time we met her on the village path. You know that when someone spits in a certain way it is a curse, so that woman laid a curse on us every time she saw us. My sister was so upset that the next time she crossed our path, she pointed her finger at the woman's womb which was swollen and pregnant, and in that instant her baby died inside her. The woman screamed and clutched her stomach and fell to the ground. I dared not help her because I knew the malignant power that there is in my touch. The next morning we had to leave the village, and her relatives followed us until the end of the road, shouting that if we had not left they would have killed us."

"But how could they do that? Their relative was at fault!" Vilie exclaimed.

"Thank you, you are the first who has said so. We know there are some in the village who think like you too but were too afraid to speak up for us. In her day my aunt pointed her finger at a man and blinded him because he was trying to rape her. She was sent away from the village and we never saw her again. Now we live here and we don't need anyone anymore but they need us. When they need us to tell them what herbs would be good for curing tumours and other ailments, they come to us with offerings. On such days, they stand at the forest's edge and call out to us and we ask for an offering. What offering? You know salt or sugar, a little something that we have a craving for and don't want to wander out to buy or steal. That is how we deal with one another. So you see, you have not been the first to wander into our territory. "

"But not every woman here is kind like you. I can see that. I can also see that your sister would like to harm me if she could. What have I done that she hates me so?"

"It is not what you have done, but what you have with you that makes her envious, and that envy creates malice and something close to hatred."

"So you know what I have with me?"

"You cannot hide it from us, Vilie. But I do not covet it like my sister does so you are safe with me." He looked directly in her eyes but could detect nothing deceitful there. She sat facing him as she said this, and he wondered how such a gentle creature as this could have been ostracised by a whole village, and condemned to live in this manner. At

that moment all that he felt for her was compassion, and
nothing of the former feelings of suspicion returned. He
grew trustful and fell asleep in the bed she had provided
for him.

THIRTY-TWO

Love and Death

"IS SHE DONE PLAYING WITH YOU?" boomed a voice at the entrance of the house. Zote had blocked the entrance and was standing at the door threateningly. Vilie rose to his feet and instinctively felt for his gun. It was not loaded but she would not know that.

"Ha! Are you going to scare me off with that? Hasn't she told you we are immune to bullets and lead?"

Her very presence was evil. She was so full of contempt for everything around her that she could not speak a sentence without ending it in a curse. Vilie tried to speak but his voice stuck in his throat and all that emerged was a hoarse sound. It was as though she had emasculated him.

"The stone is not for you. If you try to misuse its wealth, it will give you enough sorrow to regret you ever took it," Vilie warned in a gruff voice.

"Foolish man! I have no use of the wealth that the stone provides. I want much more. I want the power of battle that will avenge me against my enemies. I want nothing more than to wreak havoc upon those who threw me out of my village. To see their young destroyed and their houses in flames, their fields ablaze, that is all I seek. Only then will I be satiated."

She spat at the ground as she spoke and Vilie felt a wave of pity for the twisted soul that she had allowed herself to become. Yet he had to be careful because she was after the heart-stone and would try to take it away from him with all her strength. Zote noticed that her sister had come to stand protectively by Vilie.

"And you my dear sister, don't think your pretty ways will have any effect on him. Our kind are not meant to love or be loved. That has always been your great weakness, and the reason you are protecting him is because you have a foolish dream that you can find love with a man some day. Well, if he so much as touches you he will die from the poison in your blood. I should not have warned you. I should have let you try it and then my purpose would have been fulfilled!"

She gave a laugh at this, a laugh that was more a shriek, evil through and through, enjoying the discomfort she had caused, and then she left as abruptly as she had come. Some awkward moments passed after she left. Zote's words were like malignant seeds sown in the air – bearing fruit that was just as destructive. Vilie broke the silence first.

"Was she right about that – that you would poison me by your touch?" he asked.

Ate hung her head and answered, "Yes, that is right.

That is one of the reasons why we live away from human society."

"I don't believe her. You have a kind heart. You acted in compassion toward me, and last night you saved me even though you didn't know what manner of man I was. I think she is using your past and the past of your ancestors to condemn you. I don't believe there is an injurious bone in you. And you must not believe it either."

Ate looked up at him gratefully. Vilie could see from her expression that his words had moved her.

"Have you ever harmed anyone with your powers?" Vilie asked.

"No, I have never tried to use them on humans. Many years ago, Zote took me out and asked me to point at a young plant. I did that and in the evening, she showed to me that it was dead and completely withered. I was shocked at that and I took care never to point at a human or any living animal, not even the wild animals that sometimes wander into our village here."

"Could she have deceived you? Could it be that the same evil does not reside in you? Maybe she didn't want to leave her village alone?" Vilie pondered out loud.

"That can't be true. All Kirhupfümia are supposed to have the power of death at the ends of their fingertips."

"Have you tested it? I think you should test it. You should not just accept what people say about you. It may not be true."

Vilie's words burned deep into her heart, and she

admitted that she truly wanted to know if she could harm others with her touch. Vilie suddenly reached into his bag and pulled out the heart-stone. He held it up to the light in the room and said, "Here is the stone!" The heart-stone caught the light from the fire and reflected it back in its purple surface. He heard her gasp at the sight.

"Would you like to hold it?" he asked.

"Do you trust me to?"

"I trust you. Here," he reached out to pull her hand and lay the stone in her palm. She slid the heart-stone up and down her palm and marvelled at it.

"It's burning me a little. Just a little. It feels good. Like a cleansing." She still held the stone in her hand, her eyes closed and her whole face glowing with joy. It was so momentary that neither of them knew when it passed on.

"Ate," Vilie called her name softly. She opened her eyes.

"Ate, it is not true that your touch is malignant. I touched your hand and yet you did nothing to me. You must not continue to believe in a lie that was told to you about your past. Do you understand that?" Vilie was imploring her. "It is a lie that you cannot escape your evil nature. If you accept what others say about you, you will always remain weak. You are what you believe you are and what's more, you are meant to be more than what you are. Do you see that for yourself now? Does the heart-stone give you the power to understand that?"

A long silence passed before she replied in a very soft, almost inaudible voice,

"Yes, it does."

Vilie felt something pass through him at that response from her. He felt close to understanding the real power of the heart-stone that Kani and Subale had tried to explain to him. Was that why it was called the heart-stone? It seemed to have the power to transform the heart. He knew something marvellous had happened to Ate. He watched and saw before his very eyes – her face softened by the knowledge passing into her from the stone. There was another facet to her face. He continued to look at her face because it was mirroring all that her spirit was experiencing at that moment. It was anxiety free and it was Vilie's turn to gasp at its peaceful loveliness. When her sister Zote was spewing out her hateful words, Ate's face had turned hard and lines of anxiety and dormant fear had made her look gaunt. None of that was there now. Vilie almost dared believe that now she could face her sister's wrath and not be affected by it at all. She continued to sit by the fire holding the stone, cradling it and rocking herself back and forth in wonderment.

Subale's words came back to Vilie: *it has the power to turn the hearts of others to the owner.* Ate's hands cupping the stone, and the new found peace on her face, astonished him and kept him pondering on those words.

THIRTY-THREE

The Screaming Stone

"I KNEW A MAN WOULD COME from the village of the Screaming Stone and he would bring knowledge that all would covet. But not all would be able to use it well. You are that man, Vilie, we have waited for you a long, long time."

Ate was speaking in a dreamy voice to him.

"The village of the Screaming Stone? How do you know about that?" Vilie questioned her.

"We have access to knowledge that is not always known to men. I have knowledge of your past though I do not have any knowledge of your future. No one does except the birth-spirit, Kepenuopfü. In your ancestral village of Zuzie, there were two stones that used to scream in the evening. Mothers hid their children when the stones screamed. They covered their children's faces with their body-cloths and if they didn't have a body-cloth, they would cover it with the border of their waist-cloth to protect them from whatever evil thing the stone was emitting over the village as it screamed. They would plug their children's ears and pull them inside their houses and shut the windows and doors.

When those two stones screamed, it was always followed by war, or pestilence or sudden death. The mothers believed they were shielding their children from all that when they stopped up their ears and eyes. In later years the villagers covered the mouths of the stones with pebbles and soil and leaves. The stones were not high, not much higher than three feet, but it took a whole day of digging soil to fill up the two stones. Who knows where the openings led to, and from what secret underground chambers those sounds were spewing forth? And you buried your mother in that village and made the forest your home, but you always think of that village where your mother is buried as home, your real home, and you long to go back, at least in your dreams if not in your waking moments."

Vilie knew all that she spoke of was true. He bade her to speak on.

"You come from a long line of warriors but you have chosen to be a hunter. You trap animals for food but also protect the ones entrusted to you. Not many men can keep that balance. There was a woman in your life once many years ago. Not a woman, maybe a young girl, and she is not there now. Did she marry another?"

"No, she died a spirit-induced death. Her name was Mechüseno."

"You loved her very much."

"I did but now the forest is my wife. She provides food for me and more, she is the sanctuary I need and I am content with that."

"Perhaps you are meant for more," Ate looked at him as she said that. She had pronounced it as though it were a certainty. Vilie gave no reply.

"Perhaps you are to be the guardian of the heart-stone. The river gives the heart-stone to those who seek its blessing, but denies it to those who will use it for evil purposes like my sister, Zote. The heart-stone is also a stumbling stone, and people who don't understand its mysteries can possess it but also stumble and lose their way. But it is not the stone that makes them do that. It is their own impure hearts and their corrupted understanding that leads them to use the stone for cruel purposes. Of course you know that the stone gives cattle and wealth and beautiful women. But that is not the true purpose of the stone. It imparts spiritual knowledge to its owner. It is imperative that you guard the stone from my sister. If she gets hold of it, the only use she will have for it is to wreck the village that has done her wrong. There are good people in the village too and it is not at all right that the good should be punished for the faults of the bad ones."

"What about you Ate? Don't you want revenge on those who drove you out of your home?"

"This is my home. I feel at home here where there are none to judge me or to spy on me and accuse me of things I am not guilty of. Here there is no one to say that I caused a bad harvest or that I brought hail and lightning to destroy the crops of my neighbours. I don't hanker to go back. I was quite young when I left. I have no pleasant memories of my ancestral village that I should want to go back to it."

"I am happy to hear that for your sake," Vilie responded.

"But you have need of the stone for yourself too." said Ate looking at him with her clear eyes, "There is a dark shadow in your past and you are not quite free of it. It is black and heavy. That means there was a death you were connected to. Possibly a murder. It is very recent, a few weeks ago perhaps. Have you killed someone before you came here? Even by accident?"

"No," Vilie replied, thinking hard. "There was a killing, but I was not part of it. It was a group of hunters and I shared their shelter, and in the night the eldest brother shot the leader of the group. I was a witness to the killing and I had to run because he was about to kill me."

"Is there more to this story? I see dark clouds following you from this time."

"I was hunted by some men who believed I was the killer. I gave myself up and was eventually proved innocent. It was a terrifying time but I have put it behind me now."

"Perhaps that is what you imagine but I can see it still follows your spirit. It will probably take years before you are free of it," Ate said softly. She was still holding the stone.

THIRTY-FOUR

Ate

IN THE AFTERNOON ATE WAITED until the others had gone out to the forest to gather herbs. She said the others were all right and would not harm Vilie so long as he was her guest. But she did not want to take any risks with her sister Zote who she knew would not hesitate to kill Vilie in order to get the stone. They ate the leftovers from the night before and went out of the house. Everything was quiet for the inhabitants had all left for the forest. Ate showed him around the village. There was a communal grain pounding house with several mortars set up in a row. Each mortar had a pair of pestles, and they could see that the women had been pounding grain not too long ago. Husk lay on the floor next to some of the mortars.

"When we came here, some of our clansmen cut down trees and carved these mortars and pestles for us," she said by way of explaining how they had got there.

All the houses had gardens in the back with a few vegetables growing, chilli plants, garlic and ginger. The village had two water sources which were looked after very carefully. In the lower pool, rocks for washing clothes were lined up on the bank. Ate explained that the upper pool was only for cooking and no one was allowed to wash clothes there. In all, there were only twelve houses in the whole village. Vilie saw the ruins of an abandoned house. When he questioned Ate, she said an old woman had lived there before they came. She was the oldest of the Kirhupfümia and died some years after she and Zote came to stay. No one had bothered to dismantle her house so its ruins still stood in the village.

"Maybe we will burn it down one day," Ate said calmly. A half-stack of firewood stood by the broken door. "There's enough firewood for that." she added.

From afar, the village of the Kirhupfümia looked like any other village with the same architecture found in these regions. Tin roofs and split bamboo walls. Open yards where cattle could feed on the piles of straw in the corner. In the event of a funeral the yard would be cleared of animals, swept and prepared to host mourners. But the similarity ended there. All the neighbouring villagers knew the story of the village of Kirhupfümia so they avoided coming too close to it. Keeping a safe distance they would look at the strange women who had the power of death at their fingertips, and marvel that they led very much the same life as they themselves did. If there was any communication between the villagers and the women, it was done very carefully, so that the villagers would not incur the displeasure of the women in any way. In these communications the village would send old men or women who would know the right way to address the Kirhupfümia. There were some common questions they consulted the women on. It could be related to the sighting of the new moon. "The new moon has its legs in the air, what does it portend for us?" they would ask. Or they would enquire what was to be done if a relative had touched stones that were taboo to touch. These and other questions about spirit encounters were the themes they sought answers for. The Kirhupfümia would ask them to bring back offerings in exchange for information.

Sometimes they would be consulted on cures for fevers contracted in the forest. The Kirhupfümia would place a basket for offerings at the village gate, and when the offerings came, they would disclose names of herbs in special areas, and how to use these to cure the fevers. "Boil and use them in broth," was a common instruction, and about some herbs they would say, 'Pound and eat it raw because its power is so subtle that it gets lost in cooking.' This was a regular transaction between the women cast out by their ancestral villages, and the people who lived on in those villages. The Kirhupfümia came from different villages of course and they had a vast store of knowledge that was garnered from their respective villages. Those who came from the southern villages knew the days of festivals and they named the genna-days for the community. Those who were from the western villages had more knowledge of cures for sicknesses and how to break a fever.

"Why are you telling me all this?" Vilie questioned when they had returned to Ate's house.

"Because I trust the goodness of your heart and I know you will not use it wrongly, for profit or for commerce of any kind."

"I have no need to," he agreed.

"Knowledge is not for trading. The exchange of offerings for our knowledge is just a ritual without which the women here would feel completely isolated. So long as they feel they are useful for something, even if it is by way of helping the villages that had mistreated them, they are giving back, and in a strange way that gives meaning to their lives. If they felt they had nothing to live for they would die out here, and this village would collapse because we have no children to carry on our name."

"Can you never have children?"

"How can anything live inside us? It is not our destiny to be mothers. In a way, it is right because our race will die out of entirely natural reasons. That is, unless some are born again in another generation of ordinary parents."

Her voice was low as she said this and Vilie felt a pang of pity for her sad lot.

THIRTY-FIVE

Zote

THEY WERE BOTH ASLEEP when the attack came. Zote charged into the house screaming curses and baneful words. Ate was sleeping in the inner room and she rose first and ran to Vilie – standing before him so he wouldn't be harmed. But Zote had pounced on Vilie's bag and was holding on to it with a firm grip.

"Drop the bag now!" Ate hissed at her sister.

But there was no way Zote was going to give back her catch. Ate sprang at her and the sisters were at each other, pulling hair, scratching and hissing. Zote was the bigger of the two but Ate was relentlessly tenacious. Vilie reached for his gun but did not know what to do. Should he shoot at a human being for the sake of a stone? It did not seem right at all. So he kept the gun back and thought of what he could possibly do to stop the fight and get the stone back. The women were hurting each other and cries of pain alternated with cries of anger.

Finally Zote shoved her younger sister away with all her

might, and while she was reeling in pain, the older woman ran out of the house with the bag. Vilie ran to Ate and led her to her bed.

"Leave me, I'll be all right, take your gun out there and shoot her in the leg or something!" she shouted.

"No, it is not worth spilling blood over," Vilie said and refused to do harm to Zote.

"But we know what she will use it for," Ate argued.

"I can't shoot your sister, whatever it is, I just cannot shoot her." Ate looked helpless. He touched her shoulder and wiped her tears away. Her scalp was bleeding in spots where her sister had pulled out her hair. Vilie found some rock bee honey to put on the wounds. Her face was bruised beneath her left eye where Zote had knocked her just before she pushed her to the wall.

"We will think of something," Vilie soothed her, "she can't go anywhere tonight with that. She will have to wait for morning. I want you to rest. I will think of something."

He persuaded her to rest while he sat up and observed Zote's house. It was dark outside, a moonless night. The only light in the village was coming from Zote's house. Vilie crept up to the house and tried to look inside. There was someone moving about, and he feared that he might make a sound or step on a dry leaf, so he returned to Ate's house. He stood in the shadows and continued watching Zote's house.

There seemed to be a lot of activity going on. By the light of the kerosene lamp burning inside, he saw a figure going

from room to room, and out the house and back in again.
He wondered what she was up to. After some moments he
saw her lug out what looked like a heavy bag and leave it
by the door. Whatever it was, she seemed to be preparing
for something significant. Should he try and get the stone
back or wait for another opportunity? Zote was not like
Ate at all. She did not have an ounce of the compassion
that her sister had for her fellow creatures. He was sure
she would not hesitate to point her finger at him and blind
him or cripple him, or whatever her black powers enabled
her to do.

Vilie turned at the sound of heavy sobbing coming from
inside. He quickly went into the house. Ate was sitting up
and watching her sister's house from the opening that
served as a window.

"She wants so much to avenge herself on our ancestral
village," she said between sobs. "She has let the rage
consume her so completely that it is all she thinks of."

"Do you think we can stop her?" Vilie asked.

"Not outright but if we could follow her without her
knowledge, perhaps we could stop her from causing too
much harm to the villagers."

"Should we watch her in turns? You sleep now and
when I get tired, I will wake you," Vilie offered.

Vilie kept vigil for five hours at a stretch but nothing
more happened at Zote's house. He did not see her leave,
and all the frantic activity stopped after some time. Oddly
enough, she left the lamp burning. He debated whether

or not to wake Ate but she woke up by herself and insisted that he rest. So he went to bed and slept immediately. Ate woke him before he had slept for an hour.

"She's leaving! Vilie wake up now, we have to follow her or else we will lose her!"

His body craving more rest and sleep, he forced himself out of his stupor, and craned his ears to hear what she was saying.

Jumping out of bed, he pulled on his sandals and stood up. Remembering his gun, he grabbed it and the cache of bullets which he had taken out of the bag, mercifully before it was stolen. It was pitch dark outside. They could hardly see a few feet in front of them, but Ate knew which direction her sister had taken. They climbed upward on the road that led from the village towards the market area. Soon they came to the end of the fields and headed to the crossroads where three paths met. But when they reached Ate was confused and could not remember which path led to her ancestral village. It had been so many years since she had left. As she stood there trembling, Vilie remembered the old man's words, *take the road left, every time you come to a turning in the road, always take the road that points left*. Very confidently he took her hand and led her to the path that pointed to the left. He let go of her hand and they walked on.

All of a sudden she stopped,

"I smell her, she is near. Let us slow down."

THIRTY-SIX

New Wounds for Old Scars

NEITHER OF THEM COULD TELL how far ahead of them Zote had travelled. But the last thing they wanted was for her to suspect she was being followed. So they slowed their pace, advancing with as little noise as possible. They proceeded in this manner for several hours, and the night sky slowly got lighter. When they reached the crest of a hillock, they could see a figure in the distance carrying a load.

"That must be her," said Ate, stopping for a moment.

The load Zote was carrying had slowed her down. It was difficult to say what it was. Whatever it was, it looked heavy because she was now dragging it behind her. The noise the bag made as it was dragged along the path had obviously distracted her from their presence, and she did not seem to hear if they crackled a twig or stumbled on a stone. Vilie stubbed his toe hard on a stone and bit down on his lip to stop himself cursing aloud. Ate was the more careful walker. She stayed to the middle of the path constantly because it was well trodden.

They reached their destination before dawn. Zote had stopped just above the sleeping village so they skirted to the side of the path keeping at a distance which was hidden from view. Unsure of her intentions, they just waited silently – peering through the shrubbery. They watched her recline until she was lying on her back. Ah, so she was tired too. The two exchanged looks. They breathed softly and waited. What would her next move be? Vilie wished she would get up again and start walking. Waiting like this was worse because she was likely to observe movement behind her if she looked back. As they waited it grew brighter since it was nearly dawn. The absence of proper forest cover made them increasingly nervous as the light grew brighter. The villagers had cleared away the trees to afford themselves a good view of enemy warriors in the event of an attack. That meant Vilie and Ate could be seen by Zote if she looked in their direction carefully. They lay as still as possible under the shrubbery. Soon, they saw her moving again. She got to her feet, and began dragging her load downward towards the village.

Morning sounds rose up to them from the village. Roosters crowed, and infants could be heard crying. Mothers were rising to get their fires going for morning tea. Sounds they were both familiar with from their childhood. It was how everyday life began in the village. The clinking of water pots could be heard as early risers made their way to the water-spot to fill their pots. That tranquil picture of morning gently coming to the village was quickly shattered by Zote's shrill voice. Shrieking curses, she opened her bag and reached into it to pull out a plague of boils on the villagers. Zote seemed to have grown in stature, and looked terrifying as she stretched out her arm and threw the globules of pestilence over the village. At the same time, a swarm of rodents and lizard-like creatures sprang from her opened bag, and scurried toward the village. She shouted as she threw the plague into the heart of the village.

Total mayhem broke out in the village as the older members realised what Zote was up to. The creatures from her bag descended on the village in a black cloud. People stumbled on them and shrieked in fear. The rain of pestilence landed on several villagers, and they ran screaming into their houses as boils erupted on their skin. Zote's shrieking and the screams of the villagers filled the air in a cacophony of sound, creating even greater confusion. Men rushed out with their spears to protect their families. But they were no match for the sorceress' attack. As they sprinted to throw their spears, they were met by shafts from Zote's lightning swift fingers. The men dropped their spears and their screams joined that of the women – for the *kirhupfü* had blinded them.

Zote reached into her bag again and drew out more curses. They looked like small black stones and as she hurled them at rooftops, the thatch caught fire and the occupants ran out in utter horror. Soon the whole village was ablaze for the thatch-roofed houses were built very close together. Even the houses with old tin roofs burned just as easily, because the timber was old and dry.

The full-on attack had happened so quickly, that Ate and Vilie were paralyzed by shock. They could not think of any way to stop Zote. She looked so formidable, hovering like a mighty avenging dragon over the helpless village. They saw women and children running in despair toward the forest. The men who were blinded were being helped by other men as the villagers abandoned their burning homes, and fled for their lives. Black smoke rose and settled in a thick cloud above the village. It would neither ascend nor dissipate further. Zote slowly walked down into the burnt village, surveying the damage as if calculating the loss against the price she herself had paid for all the years she had been made an outcaste.

THIRTY-SEVEN

When Evil Meets Evil

AS THE TWO WATCHED, she went from house to house,
spitting into each doorway. There really was nothing they
could do but stand at a distance and watch the excesses
of Zote's vengeance. The three men she had blinded had
stumbled into the woods along with the rest. An old man
was crawling away, he was so old he could barely walk
anymore. He just about managed to get to safety as Zote
strode into the village. She hissed at him and laughed
when he quickened his pace in fear. Vilie was shocked
at the savagery of her nature. It was unthinkable that
this wicked figure could be sister to the gentle creature
beside him, who at this point was weeping silently at the
incinerated village.

The village council hall was left untouched because
it was in the middle of the village. The other houses had
been constructed a respectable distance from the hall.
The council hall was made of wood and had a tin roof
instead of the thatch commonly used by the older houses.

The distance probably saved it from being affected by the fire. Zote walked straight through the village and into the empty hall. The great door was open and anyone who was watching could see what she was doing. It was forbidden for women to enter it, and when the men's meetings were held, women feared to walk past the house. On ordinary days, a few men went there with their beer mugs. It was a sombre place, sparse and musty with a wide open area for the members to hold their meetings. Village disputes were settled here, but more importantly, it was the war council room where inter-village battles were planned. By entering it, Zote had defied and violated the taboo on women entering the hall.

Ate and Vilie could see her spitting at the four corners of the structure before she exited. From their vantage point, the village looked like a battlefield. Many of the houses had burnt down and collapsed, and the smoke still rose from them to hover above the village in a heavy, black cloud.

Zote appeared like a dark spirit as she shuffled around the ruins, spitting every which way. She was completely absorbed in her vengeance. When she had circled the village, she returned to the hall and remained there for the rest of the day. Towards evening, as the sky turned red, she emerged and stood at the entrance of the hall. Set off by the red glow, the charred structures and smouldering remains of other fires presented a fearful, eerie spectacle, of burning skeletons of homes and trees. As Zote stood there, some of the simmering fires seemed to rise as if refuelled by more thatch or wood. From afar it looked as though the houses were being reignited.

Vilie pointed it to Ate who immediately covered her mouth with her hand. Her eyes grew round with fear.

"What is it? What's happening?" Vilie whispered.

"Ancestor spirits!" she breathed back, "She has invoked the wrath of the ancestor spirits! They will never let her go alive!"

Lifting her trembling hand, she pointed as the flames grew in number, opening out to reveal what appeared now as tall human-like figures with long spears and shields. It was a blood-curdling sight. As the intensity of the scene grew, they could feel the heat it radiated on their uncovered faces. The spirit-warriors seemed to have assembled from the charred remains, and formed a column, marching slowly but deliberately toward the hall. Zote turned at the sound of spears. As the warrior chant began, Zote's face contorted and grew dark. She looked prepared for a confrontation. The warriors kept marching toward her, ululating at intervals but never breaking their pace. When they were nearly upon her, Ate hid her face in her hands and cried out in horror. Vilie kept watching but chose to turn his face away when Zote let out a long shriek.

Neither of them saw what happened next, but they clearly heard her horrific cries echo round the valley for what seemed like several minutes before they subsided. Ate continued to cover her face with her hands, and Vilie pulled her to him and held her till she stopped trembling.

When Vilie finally looked up, the hall looked empty but if he looked carefully he could see a heap on the ground where Zote had stood. The spirits were gone, having administered their ghastly justice. But to make their grim visit known to others, their ululations echoed around the village long after they had gone.

"The heart-stone!" Vilie whispered to himself. Where could it be?

He was divided between wanting to run down to the village to search for the stone, and his duty to look after Ate who had fainted. He couldn't possibly let he lie there senseless while he ran off after a stone. Vilie gently roused her and when she remembered where they were, she wept for her sister.

"Whatever she was, I had no other family besides her," she mumbled between sobs.

Ate dragged herself to her feet and insisted that they go down to retrieve her sister's body and the stone.

"I know you have your reasons to hate her, but she took care of me, fed me and clothed me as best she could. I want to bury her. I simply cannot leave her body behind for wild animals to use as food."

Vilie promised her that they would do as she wished, and he added that he had no enmity toward Zote anymore. At Vilie's insistence, they waited until they were sure it was safe to go down. Then they slowly walked down the path into the village.

Zote's hair was streaked with her own blood. Her clothes

were singed from the fire and the smell of smoke was so strong that it seemed to emanate from her. Even in death her hand was clasped around the stone. Vilie used all his strength to try and open her fingers but he failed. Seeing him struggle, Ate leaned down and spoke to her sister, "Let go Zote, it is of no use to you where you are now. You have no need of it there, let go!"

"She is past hearing," Vilie protested.

"She hears me, she can still hear me. Watch!"

The hand went limp, and the stone tumbled out of it and rolled to the dust.

"We are sisters, we are twin-souled," Ate mumbled as she handed the stone to Vilie.

"No, you were never twin-souled though you were sisters. Never claim that again. You and I, we have witnessed today what happens when evil and evil clash. The ancestor spirits could not tolerate her evil deed of harming both the guilty and the innocent and they took their own revenge on her. You are not twin-souled. You have never lived so as to deserve the judgement she got."

She looked up at him and nodded her head wordlessly. The two of them dragged the body outside the village area and buried her in a clearing by the forest. Vilie found some stones and heaped them over the grave as markers, should Ate ever want to find it again.

THIRTY-EIGHT

Sometimes There are No Answers

THE HEART-STONE FELT ICY COLD in his hand. He wondered why it was so. Was it because Zote had clung so hard to it even in death? And beyond death? Vilie put it into his bag and hung it on his neck, and swung it in front. From now on, nothing would part him from his bag. He would hang it around his neck even when he fell asleep, and would make sure that no one else stole the stone. He was all right but he worried about Ate. She looked spent. Fine lines had appeared around her mouth making her look older than she was. Her eyes were red-rimmed and her voice was hoarse from weeping. Should he take her back to the village of Kirhupfümia and leave her there? Strictly speaking she did not belong there. She had no power to hurt others, and if the others found out, would that not put her in danger? Yet could he take her with him? He was unsure where his travels would lead him next. And if he completed his journey and went back to his forest home, it was still no place for a young girl.

Vilie felt increasingly protective of her. He felt responsible for her wellbeing and wanted to do for her, whatever was in his power to do. She should have the company of young people her age so she has a chance at a normal life. He thought of his ancestral village. Perhaps he could repair his old house and let Ate use it as her home. His village people were not a bad lot. They could accept a stranger and let her make a home there. They could be quite caring as well. Ate wouldn't be the first outsider to the village. One day perhaps she could marry, have children of her own, and lead a normal life in the village. She deserved that.

They did not linger in the area too long after the burial, and were soon on the path they had come on – hoping to reach the village of the Kirhupfümia in good time. They needed to face the other members, and inform them about what had happened. The journey was short, and they reached the village before noon. Yet, as they went from door to door, they found the village completely deserted. "Perhaps the women have gone fishing, or off on some excursion together?" Ate asked loudly. The strange thing was that the door to each house was flung open as though they had left in a hurry.

"What has happened here?" Ate asked as she went through the mess of the neighbouring house. Clothes were left hanging on the rack and pots and pans were thrown on the mud floor as though they had been flung at something or someone.

"Look at this! They have had a fight of some sort. There

is no other reason why the houses should be in such a mess."

"How can you tell? Perhaps the owner was late and had to rush out after the others?"

"Yes, but look at this, daos flung on the floor, spears stuck into the wall? We don't do that. It is as though she had flung it at someone and missed."

Not able to solve the mystery they went to Ate's house and made food. Then they went to sleep, exhausted by their expedition. The next morning, the village was as still as a ghost village. The women had not returned in the night, and the two realised they were completely alone in the village. Ate asked Vilie to remain in the house while she went to her sister's house to investigate. Zote's house was cold and damp. There was such a sense of melancholy about it that Ate felt quite depressed. It was as though the house knew what had happened to its owner. First she stood at the door and looked in. Then she stepped inside and gingerly looked about her. Her sister's bedclothes were on the floor, and her kerosene lamp lay beside them with the glass broken. The kerosene had spilt on the floor and the bedroom reeked of the pungent smell. In the kitchen, pots were missing and none of the cups and plates were to be found. "How strange," she thought. Had someone been here and stolen Zote's things? That would be unusual because no one ever dared approach the village, and all the members had their own things so theft was unknown. And where were all the others? Why had they gone without a trace?

"Let's leave this place, Ate," Vilie implored her, as she approached him with a perplexed look on her face. "You can live in my house in my ancestral village. I will take you there myself and help you settle in. This is no place for a young girl like you."

But she was reluctant to leave. This village had been her home for such a long time. It was all she knew.

"I will lose all connection to my sister if I leave. And if she comes back looking for me and fails to find me, she will be very sad indeed."

"How can she come looking for you Ate? She is dead. You know that. We buried her, you and I."

"Oh I know that and I don't mean she will come as she was in life. But if her spirit should come to bid me a final goodbye, and find me gone, it would grieve her very much and I couldn't bear to do that to her."

"But we don't know what has happened to the others. In any case, if she returns as a spirit, she will no longer be what she was in her life, she may not remember you are her kith and kin, and that could be dangerous for you."

"I am sorry Vilie, she was family for me and I can't let her come and not find me."

So they agreed to stay on in the village until Zote's spirit returned – though it was hard to tell when that would be. Afterwards, they would pack and head for Vilie's ancestral village. If the others did not return there would be no reason for Ate to live on alone in an abandoned village.

THIRTY-NINE

Different Paths

THE NIGHT IN THE VILLAGE was amongst the loneliest nights Vilie had known. Certainly he had experienced far more frightful nights but this was different. There was a deep sense of all-encompassing sorrow about it that was almost tangible. Partly it was Ate's grief, and he felt he understood her loss. But the contagion of that grief, and the way it affected him was an experience he had never had. He felt oppressed – in a way weighed down – by the incessant atmosphere of grief. Could death be so unbearable? Why was this one death more sorrowful than the last death he had witnessed – the murder of Pehu? Why should one death be different from the other?

Vilie did not fear encountering Zote again. If her spirit returned, so be it. He knew how to manage spirit encounters much better now. Somehow he felt he would have nothing to fear from her, though she had tried her best to harm him while she was alive. "Mine is the greater spirit," he thought. He felt confident he could withstand her spirit. He only hoped Zote's spirit would not try to harm Ate.

Meanwhile, Ate was restless and paced relentlessly around the house. She had returned to Zote's house several times to see if she had missed anything. She made a note of collecting her sister's favourite waist-cloth and some ornaments. She placed these in a basket and kept them by the door. Earlier that evening neither of them had eaten much. Their apprehension over the strange disappearance of the villagers had been enough to steal their appetites. On top of that, the waiting for Zote's spirit had quite distracted them from thoughts of food. While Ate paced – checking the basket at regular intervals - Vilie took out the heart-stone and held it close to him. He asked her if they should wait at Zote's house but she said firmly,

"She is my sister. She will come to say goodbye to me."

When Zote came, it was in a surprisingly quiet manner. They saw the dark figure enter Zote's house, and for a few moments they wondered if it was one of the other women from the village. But when they looked again, they both recognised Zote - the same height, the long hair and the way she carried herself with her head held high. But she walked now with a slight hunch, as though carrying a load. She spent some time – it could have been several hours – inside her own house. Ate and Vilie could not see what she was doing but they could hear a low moaning sound – as though she were weeping. Ate finally stood up, looking as though she would go across and comfort her sister. But

Vilie raised a hand and stopped her. "It is no longer the one you know," he said. She nodded slightly and sat down again.

They waited and waited expecting the spirit to come to their house but it got up and began to leave the village. Ate was heartbroken. Before Vilie could stop her, she ran out after her sister.

"Zote, Zote! Stop, come back! I forgive you!"

"Ate!" Vilie shouted as he ran after her.

The spirit was walking on, paying no heed to them. But it suddenly stopped and turned around abruptly. That halted them both in their tracks. They drew back from it. Then it turned away and kept on walking until it reached the village gate. For the second time, Ate slid to the ground in a dead faint. Vilie carried Ate to the house and banged the door shut with his foot. Then he placed her on the bed and gently roused her.

"Did you feel it too?" she asked.

"What?"

"The sorrow – the burden of the grief she carried. I know now for sure that she regretted doing what she did, and that she met her death through it. I know she grieves losing me. But she will never lose me. I will always love her."

She had difficulty finishing what she had to say as she was so deeply grief-stricken. Vilie could not forget the heaviness that clung to the spirit. It was such a despairing hopelessness that he hoped he would never see anything like it again. He didn't say anything to Ate about it, but he felt that Zote had met with what his people called an ominous, untimely death. The spirits of those who die before their appointed time always carried such anguish with them, that it passed on to the people in their path. It was that despondence he had sensed early on that had so overwhelmed him in the early hours of the day. Now that he knew what its source was, he was anxious to leave the village as soon as day broke. He would insist on them leaving. Another night in this blighted place would be more than any mortal man could take, he thought.

At the same time he felt great pity for Ate. This was the only home she knew. When the sisters had left their ancestral village, Ate had been nine years old. She had grown up here amongst the rest of the outcast women, but everyone had treated her well. With time, her memories of the bitter departure from her home village had dimmed, and she had embraced her new life in the village of the Kirhupfümia. How would she cope with leaving for good?

FORTY

New Morning

NEITHER OF THEM SLEPT WELL. Both had been disturbed by memories – shared and unshared. Morning came but none of the women returned to the village, and they had no means of finding out what had happened to them. The women were all from different villages, and though Ate used to feel that they were her extended family, she had no knowledge of their ancestral villages. So there was no way of looking for them. In the end, they agreed that it was a futile plan, and focused instead on packing Ate's belongings. Vilie advised her not to carry utensils as they were replaceable, but he added that she should not leave behind anything of sentimental value. Ate packed some clothing and took time to look around her house to see if there were items she might miss. From the basket where she had placed Zote's ornaments and clothes, she took a few necklaces of carnelian. Her choice of an old body-cloth surprised Vilie.

"Zote was wearing this when we came away. I used to

cover myself with it at night because it had the smell of home on it. I stopped doing that after some years but I want to take it with me because it belonged to her."

Vilie nodded and waited while she packed it. Ate had very few things she wished to take with her. Vilie was concerned that she would miss something, and tried to persuade her to look again amongst her things, but she shook her head.

"If I am going to start a new life, why should I take so much of the old life with me? It would only hinder me from beginning my new existence. It would only make me long for the old life again, and that would make me miserable. I must accept that my life here has ended, and I must focus on my new life if I want it to work."

Vilie marvelled at the wisdom of the young woman, and did not say anything more. They prepared a final meal together, and having packed some food for the journey, they were ready to move. Ate locked the front door by habit though she realised it made no difference. She took one last look around the village which had been her home for eleven years, and turned to pick up her bag and follow Vilie out of the gate.

They walked in silence for some time. Ate led the way as Vilie was not familiar with the area – a fact that had caused him to stumble upon the village of the Kirhupfümia in the first place. He offered to carry Ate's bag but she insisted it was not heavy at all, so they went on their way not stopping until they had reached the top of a low hill in their path.

From that vantage point Vilie tried to identify landmarks that would help him navigate their journey. He said he could recognise trails in the westerly direction, and was quite sure that if they kept going west, they would come to the fields and from then it would not be a great distance to the forest of nettles. This cheered them and they walked at a faster pace. When they reached a large tree Ate stopped.

"I don't know the way from here," she confessed.

"Do you mean you have never ventured out further than this?"

"No. There was no need for me to travel as we got all that we needed from the village or from the offerings of salt, sugar and tea from the villagers. I was safe in the village of the Kirhupfümia, and preferred it that way. Zote was the bold one wandering out with other women, and bringing back things from the outside world. Sometimes it was just stories of their travels but these were wondrous for me to hear. That is how my life has been. I feel vulnerable without Zote around, because she always protected me. In spite of what you think of her, she truly cared for me and though we disagreed on things, we had sisterly love for each other."

"Of course she cared for you. No one is completely bad and even if they do bad things, there is still some vestige of goodness in them which can be brought out. But if you leave it too late, it gets so polluted that it feels like it's too much of an effort. That is what makes them remain where they are."

They paused to take stock of their bearings, and saw that they were not far from the valley which led to the forest of nettles. It would take less than a day's walk to reach the forest. Spurred on by this, they set a good pace and finally reached a shady tree with spreading branches where they could eat their meal. After eating they resumed their journey, walking all afternoon until the path they were travelling on came to an end where the valley began. The forest was quite close now, but Vilie thought they should find a shelter or make one for the night. They would certainly not travel by night. They could see that it would still be a very long walk to reach the thick forest cover, so they decided to camp where they were for the night.

Ate helped by cutting down branches, and dragging them to the campsite to make a shelter. This part of the woods was abundant in elephant grass which they cut to make a roof over the shelter. While Vilie was building the shelter, Ate kept herself occupied with gathering firewood. There was a small stream nearby from which she fetched enough water to make a meal. Soon the pot was boiling on the fire. After their simple meal, they sat by the fire, feeding it repeatedly with twigs and small pieces of wood. There was no real danger from small animals, but they had to look out for predators. They kept the fire burning to keep tigers away. Vilie remembered the weretiger that had attacked him. It seemed so long ago now. He told Ate he could never be sure if real tigers were still around in the area, but it would be foolish not to keep a big fire going.

Anyone spending the night in the woods would do that without a second thought.

Ate looked tired. It had been quite a day for her. Leaving her home for good, and journeying from sun-up to sun-down towards an unknown future was indeed a big thing. Vilie felt sorry for her. She had not looked back when they had climbed to the top of the hill which lay directly above the village of the Kirhupfümia. Nor had she wept again after their journey had begun. Vilie felt proud of her, and wanted to tell her so though he wasn't sure how to express it. Unable to put it in words, he sat on the other side of the fire, and began telling her about his travels. He told her about the forest home he was going back to. She looked up with interest when he mentioned that, and asked if there were any other people there. So Vilie told her about the Nepali settlement and the couple with their infant son.

"I have never carried a baby in my life. I have never even been near one because no mother would trust us with their children."

"Well, you will soon find out if you can carry babies or not," Vilie responded.

He was already planning to bring little animals for her to carry around, and be convinced that she had no poisonous powers in her. He had stopped believing long back that she was a Kirhupfümia. Now all that he wanted to do was to help her stop believing that she was the person she had believed she was all her life.

FORTY-ONE

Purgation

ATE AND VILIE HAD A PEACEFUL NIGHT, both sleeping well until the sun rose over the valley. They prepared a morning meal and ate it. After that, they packed their bags and were on the trail again. The skies were clear so they knew it would get quite warm in the day. If they reached the wooded parts of the valley, they would be able to walk in the shade of trees during the warmest part of the day. They covered the long stretch of open ground that led to the woods. There were very few trees along the way, and only when they had walked for another two hours, were they able to get to the beginning of the woods. It was just as well for the sun was beginning to beat down on them as the day lengthened. The woods stretched for some miles and were pleasant by day, though they both knew it would be cold at night. Birds sang in the trees, and squirrels and flying foxes flitted from tree to tree. The trees were shady but not thick as in the unclean forest, and the birdsongs and rodent noises made it an agreeable walk. They rested at least twice, short breaks that refreshed them and got the sluggishness out of their legs.

When they reached the end of the woods, they came to a field which seemed familiar to Vilie. He didn't want to go on. He felt heavy in his spirit at the sight of the field, though he could not fathom why. He looked around him for clues, but he found nothing. So they walked slowly to the middle of the field where a shed was standing. When they got close, with a little start, Vilie recognised it as the shelter he had stayed in with Pehu, and the hunter-brothers. It was the same spot where the drunken Hiesa had killed Pehu. Vilie shuddered.

"What is it?" Ate asked for he had gone very quiet.

"This is the place where one of the hunters killed the leader."

Vilie had told her about that incident. With wide eyes, she asked,

"Is this the shelter? Did he shoot him outside here?" Ate ran to the spot where there were three square stones and ashes from an old fire. It looked abandoned. Vilie was quite sure no one could possibly have used the shelter after the murder. It was surprising that it had been left standing. Normally the incident would be considered such an anathema that the owners would have burnt the shed to the ground.

Ate was examining the area curiously when she gave a little cry,

"It's blood! The victim's blood is still here!"

Vilie was shocked to hear this and ran over to her. Congealed blood lay in a hard brown mass next to the fireplace. No one had bothered to put soil over it. Possibly they had taken the body home, and not returned to clean up afterwards. Vilie had the strangest of feelings standing there looking at the dried blood that once flowed through a living human being. For the second time, he felt guilt, as though it had been his hand that had raised the gun and pulled the trigger. He tried to shrug off the feeling.

"Let's go. We won't be camping here, that's for sure," Vilie said to Ate. But Ate would not budge. He stood at a distance and waited impatiently.

"You have not purged yourself of guilt," she began slowly and looked over at him. "If you don't do it, it will follow you and hinder you."

"But I was never part of it. In fact, the killer tried to blame the killing on me, you know that. I have told you all."

"Think back," Ate insisted. "Did you have any share in it, even if it was in an subconscious way?"

"That's ridiculous. Why would I have wanted him killed?"

"Not like that. But did you do all you could to prevent the murder from happening?"

Her last question cut Vilie to the quick. He stopped trying to defend himself. When he did that, he could see himself standing behind the opening to the shelter, listening to the raised voices, waiting and doing nothing. He remembered how he had hesitated to join Pehu in getting Hiesa to stop drinking. Then the shot came even as he stood hesitating. But other things came to his mind. He had grabbed his bag and gun at some point between the arguing and the shooting. He had prepared to run off if anything should happen. His complete distancing of himself from responsibility and involvement became clear to him, and he felt contemptuous of his own conduct. No wonder he had been hunted by the villagers. Waves of guilt washed over him again. He had not wanted to be involved in the argument, but he had done nothing to stop it when it had been in his power to do so. Had he stepped up and done something, Pehu might have been alive today. This guilt so pierced him that he began to feel nauseous, and dropped to his knees. He stayed there mumbling a prayer for a long time. Ate came back to him with a cup of water. He drank it but couldn't swallow it. The water was so bitter it choked him. He pushed the mug away and looked up at her.

"What did you put in it?"

"I squeezed some bark juice in it. Drink it up. It helps purge your spirit of guilt," was Ate's simple explanation.

Vilie raised the mug to his mouth, grimaced and swallowed the bitter fluid.

He stood up after that, and went over to the place where Pehu had toppled over.

"I am sorry I failed you. I was a coward then. I hope you can forgive me."

He felt better for having said that, and admitting he had

been wrong in not acting in time. The very act made him feel a different person, freed of a ghost from his past. He went into the shed and rummaged around for some time.

"What are you looking for?" Ate asked.

He didn't answer her but came out with a rusty spade. He began to dig the soil next to Pehu's blood. When he had dug a deep hole he scooped up the dried blood with the spade, put it in the earth and covered it up. Then he put some stones over it in such a way that a passer-by would know it was a memorial, and hesitate to disturb it. He felt the despondence lift from his spirit. Slowly he walked away from the shed, leading them back onto the small path by the fields.

FORTY-TWO

The Nettle Forest

THEIR PATH LED THEM TO ANOTHER FOREST, one that began a few miles after the first one ended. It was evening and Vilie suggested camping at the edge of the forest to which Ate agreed. They put their bags down and Vilie went off in one direction to cut wood for their shelter, while Ate went in another direction to gather firewood. She had not been gone long when Vilie heard a series of small cries. Alarmed he ran to find her.

"What is it Ate?" he shouted.

"Nettles!" she screamed back, hopping about and stopping to rub her legs and arms. "I grabbed a good piece of firewood without seeing that there were nettles growing all around it."

"The Nettle Forest! Of course that is where we are!" Vilie exclaimed.

Ate looked puzzled and he rushed to explain, "We are much closer home now. I came past this forest which is called the Nettle Forest and I met three women here."

"Real women? Or were they spirits?"

"Oh very real women. They were harvesting nettles."

"Whatever for? How odd that anyone should harvest nettles. Ow, I've been stung so badly!" Ate rubbed her legs again.

"Sorry, let's get you out of here," Vilie said and cut away the nettle-plants in their way with his *dao*.

They got out of the wood carefully and without further mishap. The forest ahead of them was a long stretch of nettles. Vilie gathered more wood for the shelter. They didn't have enough firewood, so they quickly carried what they had to the campsite, and worked hurriedly to set up the shelter and make a fire. By the light of the fire, they pulled in more wood and stacked it on top of what they had already collected.

With the fire going it wasn't long before they could make the evening meal, and the pot was simmering with dried meat, rice, salt and some garlic that Ate had brought with her. Vilie saw her put something else in the pot.

"Dried mustard leaves."

"Excellent! It will be a real meal then," Vilie said, with some enthusiasm in his voice. "You know you can also add nettles to the pot. I have been told they are marvellous in broth."

Ate's face wrinkled with distaste at the suggestion.

"Nettles in broth? Are you crazy?"

"There's always a first time. I have been told that by

several women and therefore I happen to believe there is some truth in it. Shall I try to get some?"

"If you really want to," Ate said in a resigned voice.

Vilie sprang up and began to cut the nettles with his *dao* so eagerly that Ate had to suppress a laugh. He brought back a bunch from which they carefully picked only the tender leaves and added them to the broth. When the food was served, Vilie watched while Ate tasted her food gingerly.

"Well?" he asked. She looked up without saying anything. "The nettle taste all right?" he asked.

"It tastes a bit odd but it seems all right. I have to stop thinking of it as something that stung me and start thinking of it as food." They both laughed.

After they had eaten, Vilie made a torch out of a firebrand and cut away any plants or leaves near Ate's bed. He cut away all the undergrowth so that the ground around her bed was quite barren.

"Just making sure there are no nettles to sting you in the night," he explained.

Thankfully there were no more incidents with nettles and they both slept well. When morning came they saw that they were not alone. Women were descending on the Nettle Forest. There were at least eight or nine women coming in their direction. Vilie and Ate swiftly packed their bags, and waited for the women to reach them. Vilie greeted them first so as to allay their nervousness at the sight of strangers. They returned the greeting, and when they came closer he recognised one of the girls. She had been with Idele when he was here last. She smiled slightly, and turned her face away from his stare. The group was made up of young girls with two older women leading them. Vilie addressed the woman at the head of the first group.

"Harvesting nettle-plants?" he asked.

"Yes, this is the last day of the harvest. After this we won't be able to make use of the nettle because winter will soon be here, and that makes the plants turn brittle so that it becomes very difficult to strip the bark."

The woman looked curiously at Ate and asked, "Your daughter?"

Vilie did not expect that question and hesitated a bit and then answered, "Yes, you are right. She is my daughter though we are not related by blood."

The woman peered at Ate and asked, "Do you want to learn to weave nettle-cloth?"

Ate giggled, "Won't it sting me?"

"Not after it has been stripped and made into yarn. I could teach you. These girls are going to harvest as much as they can, and they will learn how to strip the bark and make it into yarn."

"Will you do all of that today?" Ate asked in surprise.

"No no. We will take it home and work on it over the next weeks. We have finished tilling our fields, and are waiting for the harvest, so now we have time to make nettle-cloth, and we want the young ones to learn it before we all pass away. We have already lost one of our best weavers."

"Oh that is very sad," Vilie began. "I met a woman here some weeks ago and she was very well versed in the art of nettle weaving. Her name was Idele. A woman about your age or a bit older."

"Idele died some days ago, the same person you speak of. Ah, so you met her here. That must have been her last trip because she was sick for about two weeks after the harvesting and then she died. She was a woman who never tired of doing good to others, be it a friend or a complete stranger. We are all in deep mourning, and the reason why we are here is to harvest nettle-plants and make a beautiful nettle-cloth in her memory."

Vilie was shocked to hear of the death of the woman who had been so gracious to him when they met. He had even asked her to weave him a bark-cloth, and she had said she would. That was just a few weeks ago. And now she was dead. How fragile human life was, he thought. In spite of all its striving, when death came it spared no one. He felt a little melancholy at this thought and the woman noticed it.

"She lived a good life and she was kind to all. You should not grieve her going but rejoice that she lived a beautiful life."

"I will keep that in thought in my mind. It was an honour to meet such a fine woman. I can understand the loss your society must be feeling," he said to her.

They both fell silent for moments. Presently one of the girls ran up, and asked the woman a question. As they moved away, Vilie looked around for Ate. She was merrily talking to the young girls who were harvesting nettle, and she was giving it a try. There was some giggling and some screaming, and then she returned proudly with a clump of nettle-plants in her hand.

"What will you do with that?" Vilie asked her as she approached.

"I will make nettle-cloth. They said they would teach me."

"Then we have to follow them to their village, and stay there a few weeks. It's not something that you learn in a day or two, you know." He tried to look grave as he said this.

"Can you take me to them when we have rested a few days at your house?" Ate asked.

"Certainly I can and you may learn all you want from them."

They bid farewell to the women, and walked away from the forest. As Vilie had done on his first trip, they walked very slowly and carefully on the path out of the forest. The nettle growth seemed to have thinned since the last time, but the fact was that the women had harvested close to the path so they had cut considerably into the Nettle Forest. It made walking safer for all travellers.

FORTY-THREE

The Ghost of the Tiger

"NOT LONG FROM HERE," Vilie spoke encouragingly to Ate. He could see that she was quite tired from their long walk across the valley after leaving the Nettle Forest. They had not eaten since morning, but they both agreed that they would rather save time by covering as much ground as they could, before they camped for the night. The path widened when they came to a plot of fields, and the trees grew scarce as they had been cut to make way for rice cultivation. A few trees stood in the middle of the fields to give shade on sunny days. The rest of the landscape was flat and levelled, and several fields lay across the length of it.

Vilie led the way to a shed which looked bigger than the ones he had seen before. It was newly thatched, which meant that they would be safe from rain in case of a sudden shower. The old thatch roofs allowed rain to leak in easily, and made it difficult to sleep if it rained in the night. The shed was quite big so it probably belonged to an owner who used hired workers in his fields. Vilie set his gun

and bag down and went to gather firewood. Ate wanted to
help but he insisted that she stay in the shed. He lugged
back damp wood as he could not find any that had been
untouched by the long months of rain. They found some
dry logs stacked in the cabin which they decided to use to
get the fire started.

"I sheltered in another shed on my way out, but it was
shattered by the tiger that attacked me in the night," Vilie
recounted to Ate.

"Oh was this the weretiger you told me about?"

"It was the weretiger, and I took care not to kill it though
I could have."

"Why didn't you? How close did it come to killing
you?"

"It charged me and I shot my gun to scare it off, not
to kill. If I had killed it, it would have been equivalent to
killing a man, because a weretiger is the spirit of a man,
and it is not a real tiger. The man dies shortly after the tiger
is killed."

"So that is why you did not kill it," Ate spoke
thoughtfully. "My uncle killed a tiger when we were still in
the old village. The men brought it home, and threw their
spears at it long after it was dead. My uncle had to perform
a very complicated ritual. They said it was to prevent the
mates of the tiger from returning to kill the man."

"I wonder was it the same ritual as we have in our village?
Did he have to be guarded by his clansmen at night?"

"Yes, yes," Ate said eagerly and continued, "that too and

it was taboo for him to eat certain foods for a week after the kill. When he died his grave had the tiger-killer's marker. It was a real tiger that he killed and not a weretiger."

Ate wanted Vilie to tell her again all about the tiger he had encountered, and he recounted the story. How he had fallen asleep only to be awoken by the animal's prowling outside his shed, and how it threw itself at him, but fell to the ground when he had sidestepped. He narrated how he had tried speaking to it the second time it came, and calling it by the name of the man to whom it belonged.

"So the tiger answered to the name of the man?" Ate asked.

"Not in an audible way but he recognised human speech, and certainly he recognised his name as I used it, and the rebuke I made as a fellow clansman. I did not appeal to him, you understand? I rebuked him. He never bothered me after that."

"If it comes tonight I shall point my finger at it," she said fiercely. Vilie had to laugh at Ate's attempt to look intimidating.

"No, you will not. If it comes, I shall speak to it as before. I shall rebuke it. Have you forgotten that you have no evil power in your finger? It was your sister who kept you deceived. Remember that kindness and cruelty cannot live together. One will always have to give way to the other."

"Am I powerless now?" she asked.

"No, it is not like that. You are so much more powerful now than you have ever been before. You are the new person that you believe you are, and that new person is full of life, not death. Your power will help to build up, not destroy."

"Oh, I never thought I was capable of helping others."

"That was the old you. You are a new you now so everything is the opposite of what you used to be."

"So much to learn," she said almost under her breath.

Vilie stoked the fire, and added some of the damp wood so it would dry and burn later. Smoke rose up thickly from the fire. He didn't bother blowing on it, but waited for the damp to evaporate. Earlier they had used most of the dry wood to make supper.

"Shouldn't you get to sleep now?" he asked Ate.

"I want to wait to see if he will show up."

"Who? Oh the tiger? Why should he show up when I gave him the fright of his life the last time we saw each other?" Vilie laughed.

Ate kept sitting by the fire saying she was not sleepy yet, so Vilie went to lay on his side of the shed, his gun close by him.

The fields outside had their own sounds. Night insects cheeped from the edge of the fields. From the water bodies came the call of frogs. Ate listened attentively to every sound. She could hear jackals howling, but it was a distant sound. She sat by the fire for a long time peering into the dark night. Sometimes she saw shadowy figures running across the fields. Some of these were small foxes scavenging in the fields. But what were the larger forms that swiftly appeared and disappeared from her view? Or was she imagining things? If she gazed intently she saw blurred shapes that looked like gauzy sheets moving in the wind. The shapes came together and moved apart in a regular pattern. Perhaps they were plastic sheets a farmer had left out in the field, Ate thought. Suddenly one of the shapes began to move. Ate lifted her head to get a closer look. The shape was unmistakably running towards the shed.

"Vilie!!" Ate's scream was the high-pitched terrified cry of a little girl.

Vilie woke immediately, his hand on his gun as he sat up and tried to see what was happening.

"It's a tiger!" she had no time to say anything more.

The white figure was speeding up to them. Vilie cocked his gun rapidly, but realised in the last half second that this was no real tiger. *Sometimes the struggle is not against flesh and blood, but against spiritual powers which you would be quite foolish to defy with gunpowder.* He heard the old man's voice as clearly as if he were standing by his side. What now? He asked despairingly. *Use the name*, came the answer so clearly it seemed to pound over the fields like a great drumbeat. Ate paralysed by fear was right in its path as the white tiger pounced. For a moment they were both mesmerised by the beauty of the animal, muscle and sinew and white fur stretching out above them blocking the night sky from view. The sudden reminder that it was springing in attack made Vilie shout, *Kepenuopfü zanu tsie latalie!* The tiger's claw sank into Ate's shoulder and she screamed in fear and pain. Vilie repeated the command to the tiger to be gone. He was shouting the name at the top of his voice. Yet the tiger came at them, roaring and towering over them. Vilie would not give up. He fought for the two of them, he fought back Ate's fear as well, knowing that the slightest sign of fear would make the spirit gain ground. For the third time he used the name, and then the tiger crumpled before their eyes, dissolving into mist and sulphurous fumes, no sign of its might visible any longer. The pair sank to their knees in relief. They were breathing heavily from the encounter with the tiger-spirit.

Minutes went by as they waited, but the spirit-tiger did not resurrect itself. However, there were other matters to attend to. Ate was experiencing great pain in her clawed shoulder. She groaned and lifted her hand to her shoulder where the tiger had sunk its hard nails into her flesh, and felt something wet sticking to her clothes.

"Vilie!" she exclaimed in surprise. Vilie turned around to look, and found blood trickling down from two deep holes in her shoulder where the tiger's nails had punctured her skin. Swearing beneath his breath, Vilie quickly opened his bag to retrieve the powdered herbs he was carrying. He staunched the blood flow with a paste of *vilhuü nha* and despite Ate's protests, he covered the wound with herb-paste made of *tierhutiepfü* and bound it up with cloth.

How could a spirit-tiger draw real blood was the question troubling their minds, but they were exhausted from battling the tiger. There was no easy answer to that. That was a question for the seer to answer.

FORTY-FOUR

Death is Unquiet

THE NEXT MORNING ATE INSISTED THAT THEY LEAVE as quickly as they could. She didn't want any more encounters of the kind they had had. They left almost as soon as they woke, their bags hurriedly packed and slung upon their backs. Vilie had not checked if they had left anything behind, but they had not unpacked the contents of their bags except the food items. Now it was just a day's walk to the Nepali settlement. Whatever item was of importance, they had all those with them. They hurried out of the shed and walked toward the main path.

Vilie glanced over at the spot where the tiger had fallen before it vanished. The grass was trampled, and pushed down as if it had not been an insubstantial being. He worried about Ate's wound. It could very well get infected and fester for days. That would not be good at all. The best thing would be to take her to the village and have it attended to. She insisted on carrying her own bag, but Vilie would not allow it. Leaving the shed behind, they walked until they came to the end of the fields. The forest ahead was all that separated them from the next human settlement. Their pace had considerably slowed because Ate's injury gave her much pain when she walked faster. Any sharp movement aggravated the pain, and she was forced to walk much slower than she liked. Vilie wondered what he could possibly give her to alleviate the pain. He had no tobacco on him after the strange experience of losing a liking for it. Native tobacco was a good cure for wounds. Tobacco paste on open wounds could stop blood flow and was often used by villagers on wounds. The *tierhutiepfü* was a blood purifier. He had first staunched the blood with *vilhuü nha* before he applied the herb paste on her wounds. What Ate needed was some *anacin* to alleviate the pain. They stopped and took breaks when it was too painful for her to carry on.

In the afternoon, the sun was directly above them – radiating heat with unusual intensity. Vilie was walking in the lead when he heard a dull thump behind him. He turned around. Ate had fallen to the ground, and a red stain was growing on her shoulder where they had bound her wound. Vilie instantly dropped the bags and gun and lifted her up. He found a green patch of grass beside the path and carefully laid her down. She was cold to his touch, and unresponsive.

"Ate! Ate you can't die on me!" he shouted wildly as his efforts to rouse her failed.

He grabbed their bags and desperately looked for the

canteen. The boiled water was still warm from the morning. Vilie had to pry open her mouth to get some water inside. The drops trickled uselessly down the side of her mouth. Vilie was at his wits' end. Nothing he did was working. He rubbed her hands and legs, trying to warm her cold little fingers which were stiffening. He soaked a cloth in water, and wiped her face and throat repeatedly. Still there was no response from her. Vilie began to fear the worst. He felt stabbing pangs in his heart as he held her lifeless body. Frantic now, he laid her back on the grass and jumped back onto the path, and began to run back and forth, stretching his neck to scan the furthest points at both ends of the path. He saw no one, they were all alone, and his despair began to turn to desperate rage.

They had been there for what seemed like an eternity. The sun bearing down on them made her pallid skin look bloodless. At that point, Vilie realised that it would be humanly impossible to bring her back. He rushed to his bag and retrieved the heart-stone. As he squeezed it with all his might, his fury was directed at the spirit-tiger who had killed her. Vilie summoned all his knowledge of the supernatural in a last effort to battle her back to life.

Over her unmoving body, he began in a quiet voice to speak what he knew. The adrenaline in his muscles made his voice vibrate, but he desperately tried to focus his words.

"Sky is my father, Earth is my mother, *Kepenuopfü* fights for me! Take your hands off her!" He said it only once and got up. He paced like a warrior back and forth along the path. He was addressing the spirits of darkness directly, commanding them to let go of her spirit. The sun – ablaze on Vilie's forehead – seemed to grow in intensity. He hurled out challenges to the spirits. At one point he felt the urge to run in every direction, shouting loudly every which way.

The sun suddenly disappeared behind clouds, and the air cooled and dark clouds began to swirl above the spot where he stood. All at once, the forest sounds gathered and turned to a perpetual hiss that grew and magnified themselves as they drew closer. For a moment, Vilie felt that perhaps he was in over his head, and should stop what he was doing. The heart-stone hadn't changed, but he knew he was invoking evil. He continued to pace, staying close to Ate's motionless body. He made his heart strong and with his hands he motioned as if pushing back the now ear-piercing hiss that surrounded them. He felt his faith being mocked, not tested, but like a ship buffeted by stormy waves, it was being pummelled. His ears began to throb with pain as the sound thrashed against him. But he pushed back and felt a renewed sense of strength as he did that – now focusing all his energy on protecting them. He would go all the way, even die if need be, but he would never submit to their oppression.

The battling was vicious, neither side giving in. Above the solitary sound of Vilie's shouting, one could hear the grunting and the snarling of the spirits. He used words to bind them, while they used incoherent noise to terrify him, discordant sounds and intimidating growling ending in cackling cries that threatened to burst his eardrums. His gun lay useless on the ground. Gunpowder was no weapon against these forces. Nevertheless he picked it up and shot it off in the air, shouting at the spirits to beware. There was silence after the gunshots. But the attacks started up again, and the spirits now revealed their horrible shapes to him. Some of them were red-eyed and bloodied with long claws, while others were figures like the widow-women. The women cackled and came after him. Vilie saw that the spirit tiger was crouching behind them, but it did not seem terrifying at all beside these horrific spirits. When Vilie recognised the widow-women, he shouted the name again.

"*Kepenuopfü zanu tsie tuomhatalie!*"

The stone seemed to grow in his hand. He shouted these words many times, and in all directions – turning in a fury as if multiplying the sound of his own voice into that of many. As he spun his body, he closed his eyes. Though he was shouting as loudly as he could, he could no longer hear his own voice, only the echoes bouncing off the wall of trees a short distance away.

He fell to his knees, and hung his head over Ate's body. As if in a horrific dream, Vilie felt he had gone mad – that he had lost his senses. His eyes still closed, he realised he had lost his hearing. His throat was dry. He coughed several times, but only heard the thumping sound of his own fist upon his chest. He felt for Ate's hand and placed the heart-stone in her palm. Vilie felt a cold breeze sweep over them. The sun had long passed, and it had been dark for some time. Though he could open his eyes, he kept them closed – unwilling to accept that perhaps he had become delusional, and had been hallucinating. Suddenly he heard a faint sound as if coming from a distance. He slowly lifted his head but there was silence. He quickly felt for his gun and picked it up. When Vilie opened his eyes it seemed to make no difference – they were in total darkness. The sound came again. Vilie looked down as he felt a small movement at his feet.

"Ate!" Vilie sprung to her side, "Ate cough again please, that is the most beautiful sound I have heard coming from you. Ate please cough!"

Ate opened her eyes and looked up.

"Oh, have I been sleeping long? I feel so tired!"

"You are all right or you will be all right dear girl. Oh precious one, you must rest again."

Vilie was slowly regaining his hearing, the sounds increasing in volume and becoming sharper with every passing moment. It made him nervous. It seemed as though all around them the sounds of the forest had greatly intensified. At the same time, the dark clouds began to slowly pass away. They could now see each other's faces in the growing light.

"What happened? Did I faint?" Ate asked in a much stronger voice.

She sat up still holding her bandage with one hand. As

she brushed off the leaves from her hair, she noticed she had been holding the heart-stone. She glanced at Vilie.

"Yes you did, but I let you rest and here you are, fine and raring to go!"

"Did I really faint? I vaguely remember hearing you shout as I was waking up. Why do I have this stone?"

Vilie saw there was no way of keeping the truth from her.

"Actually, you slipped away for some time, maybe a few hours. It feels as though it was all a terrible dream, but I battled spirits that came initially as a hissing sound from the forest. I could see them in their horrible shapes, and they were wrestling with me over your life. I held the heart-stone in my hand, and it gave me strength. I shouted to the spirits using – His name. There were so many of them. I think they were emboldened by their numbers. First, I was completely terrified and my heart felt like stone, but I also felt so much anger at your death that I began to fight back in a rage. I think I may have gone a little crazy, actually. But I know He helped me, the creator deity helped me. His name was my weapon."

Vilie's voice was low at the last sentence. Ate could hear how weak his voice had become. She could see he had expended a great deal of physical and spiritual energy in his efforts to save her.

"I'm so sorry for all that has happened."

"Don't say that! It was not as though you brought any

of this upon yourself! The spirit-tiger took your life, but *Kepenuopfü* brought you back to life."

"You fought for me to live. You knew what to do, and you saved me – again!"

"Hey, I didn't do it alone. In fact, I could never have done it alone. Do you know I was so frustrated I took out my gun and shot it off? Even though I knew quite well gunpowder is useless against spirits. The heart-stone seemed to be speaking to me, though I had moments of stubbornness. It gave me courage, and when I used his name again and again I felt my small, weak voice becoming strong – even magnified! It all seems like a dream now. At one point I felt that perhaps I was being a complete fool. I lost my sense of hearing, and I could not bring myself to open my eyes to see your lifeless body. Oh, how wonderful it was when I heard you cough! You came alive! I tell you that cough is the happiest sound I have ever heard!"

Ate got up slowly and looked around her. The darkness had completely passed as they spoke and though the sun had set, it was still light.

"The only thing I recall is slipping into a great darkness. I felt as though I was falling, and falling – like you said, as if in a dream. I could not speak or move or breathe. The darkness was enfolding me, and the sense of despair and desolation was so overwhelming. I have never known that before or anything close to it so it's hard to describe. To think that it was all real, and that I have come back from that! I almost cannot believe it!"

"It was not your time to die. It was the spirit-tiger forcing death upon you. That is why it felt like such a desolate place. I think it was trying to pull your spirit over to their side. That is how they would do it. Rest some more," Vilie urged, "we don't have to go now."

"No. The sooner we get out of here, the safer I will feel."

Vilie remembered the wound which had caused all the trouble.

"Can I take a look at your shoulder?" he asked.

"Sure." Ate took off her cloth to show him the spot. Vilie put his hand on it and drew it away with a start.

"Your skin there is frozen! Are you feeling cold?"

"Yes, a bit."

He looked at the puncture marks, but they had closed over. Only the slightest of scars remained. It was as though the whole encounter had never happened. A waking nightmare that anyone might have trouble believing, themselves included, except for the two silver scars on Ate's left shoulder.

FORTY-FIVE

The Heart of Man

THEY FOUND SHELTER FOR THE NIGHT in a wayside shed. Getting up before dawn they continued their journey. The previous day's incidents now seemed like things of the distant past, but Vilie could not help feeling physically exhausted. They had slept only for a few hours, and they were both so tired as though their bodies had lost track of time. They also knew full well that they were too exposed where they were. Not wanting to linger, they quickly went on their way with only a drink from the canteen. Ate showed little sign that she had in fact lost her life some hours ago. She was walking at a steady pace, and there was no more pain in her shoulder, although she still felt some soreness.

Their path led them through a thicket of trees that were not very tall, but they provided good cover. Small animals scampered around in this part of the forest, but it was not likely that they would meet bears or tigers, as it was not a densely forested area. There were a few native oak trees which were not as tall as the silver oak that grew abundantly on the way to the village. This was the season for wild fruits to ripen. They saw that wood creatures had been feeding on the sweet and sour, yellow fruit of the native *Mezasi.** The over-ripe fruits had accumulated on the ground, emanating a strong fermented smell. That was the scent that greeted them as they walked through the foliage. It had drawn squirrels and other animals such as bats and monkeys. Vilie knew that deer habitually came here to feed on this fruit, but he had not seen any for a long time.

There were fewer birds here than there were in the fields. That was odd. Possibly the birds had grown wary of young boys with their slingshots who were quite accurate. After some time on the trail, they came to the plantain trees. The plantains were wild but bore fruit. On some of the trees, ripe bananas hung down within reach.

"Oh, can I try some?" asked Ate.

"Well, if they are the wild sort they are not really edible but you can try your luck."

She ran to the nearest plantain and plucked two. They were so ripe that the fruit was almost bursting its skin. Ate bit off a bit and tasted it. It was good and sweet.

"Here, they are good" she offered, but Vilie refused.

They kept walking through the plantain grove until the vegetation grew scarce and smaller trees appeared.

"Nearly there," Vilie said.

---

* Mezasi: June plum or Tahitian apple, *Spondias dulcis.*

"Your house already?" Ate asked in surprise.

"No, that is still some way off. We will stop at the Nepali settlement tonight, and I will find out how things have gone in my absence."

They had reached a clearing now, and Ate could make out the outline of the roofs of the two small sheds. The third shed lay behind the two in front. They were solid structures of wood which were made to last, unlike the bamboo structures in the fields which had to be replaced every two or three years. When they got closer, they saw some chickens running around in the clearing, and the two dogs began to bark at them. But there was no sign of the human occupants.

"Krishna!" Vilie called out, expecting the woodcutter to run out any moment to greet him with his broad smile.

There was no response.

"That's odd. Perhaps they have gone to the market to buy provisions. Let's go into the house and rest."

He led Ate into the first house which belonged to Krishna and his wife. The interior of the house was dark, and they stood at the door and peered into the darkness. The shed was technically just one long room, but Krishna's wife had hung a cloth across the middle of the room so that she had her kitchen in the first half, and the privacy of a bedroom in the other half. When they came visiting, Vilie and the other guests either sat outside on the porch or in the kitchen. They never entered the bedroom area.

The hearth was cold. That was strange because they

would have covered a firebrand with ash if they had gone to the market. The firebrand would help them start up the fire again when they were back. But the hearth looked like no fire had been made in it for some days.

"What a smell!" Ate exclaimed. "Can't you smell it?"

"What?" Vilie paused. "You're right. It's a strong smell. And most unpleasant. Wonder what it is?"

Vilie reached for Ate's bag, and hung it up along with his own bag on a nail.

"I'm going to make a fire and make us some tea."

As he spoke, he looked around the hearth for a matchbox and slivers of wood. In a minute he had the fire going, and also lit the kerosene lamp to brighten the dark interior.

"You hear that?" Ate asked.

"What now?"

"Like someone whimpering. Come here and listen. I can hear it so well from here."

Vilie came close to where Ate was sitting. He stood quietly and listened. Indeed there was a faint sound. It was a whimpering as she had said, but even fainter than that. What could it be? And where was Krishna? It was unusual that he would just go off when Vilie had put him in charge of the work of the Forest Department. And what was that whining sound that they kept hearing?

"I'm going to investigate. Something is not right around here. It is not like Krishna to go off like this."

Vilie picked up his gun and pulled the curtain aside slowly. Neither of them was prepared for the sight that met their eyes. Krishna and his wife were lying on the floor. There were deep cuts on Krishna's scalp. Coagulated blood lay on the floor. The woodcutter must have been struck several times from behind. His wife had clear stab wounds on her chest and throat. Krishna lay face down, while his wife was on her back.

"Oh God! Who could have done this?" Vilie cried out in shock.

He bent to examine the bodies. It was obvious that the two had been dead for some days. But where was the baby? There was no sign of the baby. The whimpering came again from a corner of the bed. Underneath the bedclothes they found the child, lying on its chest and barely alive. Vilie scooped him up carefully and gave him to Ate. She took him without any protest, and quickly took him to the kitchen and tried to warm him by the fire.

"Who could have done this terrible thing?" Vilie thought out loud as he opened the windows to air out the room.

He scanned the valley and forest, and then he searched the ground for foot prints or any sign of struggle. His first instinct was to rush out and look for the killer, but he knew he had to wait. He walked into the kitchen to see how Ate was faring with the child. She had placed water on the fire, and continued to hold the baby closely. Vilie fanned the fire. and brought the water to a boil. Then they cooled the water and carefully fed it to the baby. The child's eyes were shut fast and he was very weak. Vilie looked for powder milk in the kitchen, and found a small half-empty container. He took water in a cup, and mixed a few spoonfuls of milk in it, and handed it to Ate. It took a long time to get the baby to voluntarily open his mouth to drink, it was so clear that the child had narrowly escaped death.

"Not too much at a time," Vilie said gently, "let him drink at intervals."

Ate alternated in feeding him milk and water. All the while, she held his little body close to her chest and warmed him. The baby was nearly frozen when they found him, but now he was responding to Ate's care. Vilie gently rubbed his tiny feet. If the baby remained responsive, the three of them would go to his house, and then he would proceed to the village to inform the authorities about the twin murders. Vilie kept the fire burning, and he went outside leaving Ate to care for the baby. He inspected the other two sheds to see if he could find any clues as to what happened. But the sheds had not been lived in since the last time he was here. He remembered Krishna saying his neighbours were working at another log camp. So that left only one possibility. The couple must have been murdered by a complete stranger, or even by someone who knew them. It could have been anyone, a hunter, a woodcutter, just about anyone who had some business in the forest. Vilie concluded that they must be the only ones who were attacked. Vilie returned to the house. He examined the baby, and felt that they could risk taking him to his house. Ate wanted to carry the baby, so Vilie covered him well, and then placed him on Ate's chest wrapping an extra shawl around them both. He then tied the ends of the shawl securely behind her back. Bolting the door of Krishna's house, the three of them slipped quietly out of the Nepali settlement, and headed for Vilie's forest home.

FORTY-SIX

Uneasy Homecoming

ONCE AT HOME, VILIE QUICKLY WENT about making sure there was enough food for the next two days. He planned to let Ate and the baby sleep in his room while he used the guest room. But he wanted to make sure they would be comfortable when he was away. Once he had reported to the village, the village council would come to do the investigations and bury the bodies. He hoped he would not have to stay longer than a few hours at the village. Yet even as he was mentally preparing for the journey, a thought emerged and kept troubling him. Would Ate and the baby be safe in his absence? What if the killer was still roaming around in the woods? He hadn't considered that, and he realised he could not leave them here on their own. It didn't take him long to decide it was best to take them along with him to the village. They would do that as soon as it was morning.

Ate had not let go of the baby from the time Vilie put him in her arms. She even refused help when Vilie offered to carry the baby for some time so she could eat her food in peace. When she fed the child a second time, it fell asleep and slept so heavily that her arm ached, and she finally laid him on the bed. His little face looked pinched. How was it that he survived such a horrific massacre – and held out two days without food or water? It was nothing short of a miracle. In a way it was a blessing he was too small to understand what had happened to his parents. Had the killer been aware of the child? Surely he didn't just start killing them.

Krishna was a strong man. He was not tall, but he was very strong, and easily lugged around newly sawn logs to be sectioned into planks. From his youth, he had grown used to the forest life of hard labour that built up one's muscles, and kept one very fit. If the killer had attacked him head on, Krishna would have given him a good fight. The blows that had killed Krishna had been delivered from behind, obviously the work of a man who used stealth as a weapon. But, what was the motive? Vilie tried to picture a variety of scenarios, but was at a loss for a motive or cause. It seemed so meaningless to kill people who struggled for a livelihood, and were not likely to have money in the house. Could a quarrel have broken out between host and guest? And was the woman killed too because she could have given away the identity of the killer? It was all quite incomprehensible.

They ate in silence. When Ate finished she rose to take Vilie's plate, but he bade her sit down.

"I am going to take both of you with me tomorrow morning to the village to report the crime."

Ate thought it over for a bit and agreed it was best they go with him.

"As long as I don't know the whereabouts of the killer, I am not willing to let you stay here alone, and risk being attacked."

"No we should not risk it. Do you know why your friends were killed?" she asked.

"I haven't the faintest idea," Vilie replied, "This is the first time we have had such an incident in the forest. I can't imagine why anyone would want to kill them. They were fine people, no malice in their hearts toward anyone."

"I am sorry. You knew them for a long time, didn't you?" she asked.

"Some six or seven years. The wife joined him three years ago. Krishna helped me build the second room here. He sawed the planks for me and carried them over on his back. It's so meaningless that a good man like Krishna should die like that."

Vilie's voice cracked, and he put his head down. He had been too shocked by the killings to grieve. Tears came now as he talked to Ate about Krishna.

"And the wife was as hard working as him. She would join him in sawing logs and cutting planks before she got pregnant. What evil person would kill people who are trying to live their lives the best way they can without ever harming anyone?"

'"It can't end like this," she said. "Those who do ill to others will always pay in the end."

Vilie bade her go to bed while he went to the guest room and tried to sleep. The killings had taken all the pleasure out of coming home, and he did not show Ate around the house as he would have on a happier occasion. Still, things were pretty much the same as when he had left them. That meant that there had been no visitors in his absence. The bedclothes were just as he had kept them, folded and laid on the shelves, ready for use. He had tossed an army jacket on the chair and it still lay there. How long had he been away? A month? Six weeks? And so much had happened to him in that time. So many deaths too – as if there were some sort of sudden cosmic disequilibrium that needed to be rectified by claiming innocent lives.

What would they do with the baby? Some decision would have to be made soon. What would he do with Ate? She seemed to be bonding very well with the baby, and he wondered if it was a good idea at all to separate them from each other. Ate seemed to have a natural talent for child-caring, and knew all the right things to do to alleviate the child's discomforts. Vilie could not keep her here either, that was obvious. If she stayed it would have to be a completely different arrangement – possibly as his wife, something acceptable like that. His daughter? Certainly he felt like a father to her, after all he was twenty-eight years older. And in spite of all the tenderness he felt toward her, he had never considered her as a spouse. In fact, that was not something he had desired for a very long time. At the same time, he knew there would be opposition if she were to live with him as his foster daughter. He would have to sort out all those questions. For now, however, the Nepali killings were too big a matter to allow him to think of anything else.

FORTY-SEVEN

The Village

THE BABY WOKE THEM up in the morning. He wanted to be fed. Vilie made the fire and boiled water so that Ate could prepare the milk. When the three of them were ready, they left for the village, carrying with them the things they would need for the long trip. They brought milk, extra clothes, and a carrying cloth for Ate to bind him on her back.

It had been three years since Vilie had been to the village. After his mother's death his visits had grown less frequent, and a whole year would pass before he felt any necessity to return. The only relatives he had there now were his two paternal aunts. Neither of his aunts had married, and they lived in their ancestral house close to the village gate. He felt strange each time he returned. He remembered everything as it had been when he was a child and later a young man. But every year that he returned he found things had changed a great deal more than he expected. The youngsters he remembered as adolescents were married, and the girls had become matrons. The men in his age group were now responsible members of the village council, and would be found sitting in on disputes over land and fields and water. Most of all there were the deaths. Every time he visited the village, his aunts would give him a long list of the people who had died – clansmen, or men his age, or old women and young mothers. The longer he stayed away, the longer became the list of the dead. It seemed to him that many more people were dying than he could recall.

As they set out, Vilie tried to tell Ate as much as he could remember about the village, warning her as well that he had been away for many years so there might be more changes than he was aware of. Ate walked by his side carrying the sleeping baby on her back.

"I can't remember much of my ancestral village because I was so young when we left. I had a little girl to play with but we lived some distance from each other. Zote and I lived with our aunt, and our house was a little away from the main village. I think that was deliberately done back then."

"I think they do that in every village," Vilie agreed.

Though he remembered stories told of Kirhupfümia in his home village he had never seen one. There was an old unmarried woman who was rumoured to be a Kirhupfümia, but Vilie could not be sure if that was just malicious gossip. He explained to Ate how he felt more like a stranger than a member of the village on each visit. The younger people did not know him any more so they would not greet him, as they would have greeted any other older member of the village. Instead they would stare at him, and murmur amongst themselves asking each other if they knew who the stranger was. Sometimes old friends of his would recognise him, and tell their children to greet him. That was how it went.

Twice they rested and heated water to make milk for the baby. Ate thought he was ready to try some solid food, but Vilie wanted her to wait a few hours more as the baby had been starving after his parents were killed. He was already looking quite well under Ate's care. Gurgling happily he smiled up at her as she fed him spoonfuls of milk. The path widened when they were close to the village. There was a steep climb to the entrance and they saw people milling about in the square. There were more people than usual. The gathering was watching a wrestling match taking place within the square. The entry of Vilie, Ate and the baby did not go unnoticed, and people turned from watching the players to look curiously at the trio.

Vilie took the path that led to his aunt's house where he intended to leave Ate and the child. They felt eyes following their every move. Suddenly Vilie saw a face he recognised in the crowd.

"Kelethuzo! *Vizonhie?*"* He called out in greeting.

Kelethuzo, a tall man who stooped slightly, turned around in surprise and shouted back his reply. The others standing next to him milled around him to ask who it was.

---

* vizonhie: all well?

Soon, more shouts went up, and Vilie stood waving and responding to people. He pointed to his aunt's house and turned in that direction. They understood that he was first going to greet his relatives. Both Vilie and Ate knew that though the villagers were polite, they would be eager to find out the identity of the woman and child accompanying their fellow villager.

At the entrance to his aunts' house Vilie called out loudly, "Anyie* Selono! Anyie Peleno!" There was an answering shout from inside. They heard something clattering to the floor and chickens being chased off before a white-haired old woman emerged. Behind her stood another equally old white-haired woman, watching them carefully.

Vilie walked right up to them.

"Anyie it is Vilie, your nephew!"

"Vilie! Vilie!" They both exclaimed happily and bade him come in. They saw Ate was with him and extended their invitation to her as well.

"Vilie-o! I thought I would never see you again before I died!" declared Selono, the older of the two.

"I too – I thought he had died somewhere because it has been so long since we saw him," Peleno added.

"Is this your wife? Is that your child?" came the questions rapidly.

Vilie explained who they were in as simple a manner as he could. His aunts were astonished.

---

* anyie: paternal aunt.

"*Hou!* What a terrible story."

However, he did not tell them everything about Ate. They didn't need to know, and no one else needed to know her background. That was what he had decided on the way here. He knew that there were people in the village, who could ruin lives with their gossip and half-truths. Ate could do without that. She deserved a better life after all she had gone through. He was still not quite convinced she would find it here. The two aunts bustled about, busying themselves and preparing food for their visitors. While Selono measured rice into the pot, Peleno went to the brew-vat, and came back with two medium sized mugs of brew for the younger people. They were obviously very pleased with the visit. When she had the rice going, Selono waddled off to the back of the house, and went into the chicken shed and returned with two eggs. Proudly she showed them to Ate.

"One for you and one for your child," she said, and then she washed the eggs and popped them into the rice pot. She let them cook some minutes in the boiling rice pot. Selono tested an egg with her spoon and was pleased with the *pling* sound. "Ready! " she said as she scooped them out and laid them in a bowl.

"There! You can open it and feed one to the little man," said Selono.

Ate had put the baby down on a low cane chair. She took the proffered bowl and proceeded to open the soft boiled egg.

"Should I give him all of it?" she asked Vilie.

"See if he wants it and if he does, it shouldn't do him any harm." So she mixed it with a bit of rice and fed the baby. They were all amazed at the child's rapid recovery. The more they fed him, the more he wanted to eat. The pinched look in his face was slowly disappearing, and he gurgled happily as Ate spooned egg into his mouth.

"What's his name?" asked Peleno.

Ate and Vilie looked at each other and began to laugh. The aunts looked at them in surprise.

"He doesn't have a name, not one that we know of," Ate confided. Vilie tapped Selono on the shoulder.

"Well, that is a job for you then. You can think of a name for him and we will call him by that name. And while you are doing that, I will go and meet the council members and report the crime to them. That is what we came here for, though our reunion has almost driven that out of my mind."

"You must eat and go. You have been travelling for so long," Selono insisted.

She got up and took out a plate and began to serve food before Vilie could protest. He sat down and ate her food. It was warm rice and meat with mustard leaves and ginger.

"Wonderful. You haven't lost your touch, Anyie," he said between mouthfuls.

"Thank you. You should come by more often to sample my craft, nephew. Not just once in every three years," she cleverly quipped. They all laughed at that.

After the meal, Vilie stepped out and began to construct in his mind the story he would tell the council.

The women kept sitting in the kitchen taking turns holding the baby. Ever so often Peleno piped up with a name,

"Neiphretolie was our uncle's name. Should we give him that name?"

The other two thought about it, and shook their heads. The aunts came up with several names that afternoon – most seemed to already be taken, or simply didn't sound right.

"Vitohulie, is that a good name? Do we know anyone by that name?"

They didn't know anyone by that name so they finally agreed to call the baby by that name. It was shortened to Vibou. The women called him by it repeatedly and he seemed to respond, turning his head every time he heard his new name.

FORTY-EIGHT

The Stone

THE COUNCIL MEMBERS LEFT IMMEDIATELY after Vilie delivered the news. He asked if he could be of assistance, but they could see how harrowing it had been for him and they wanted to spare him further pain. Refusing his help, they set off to bury the unfortunate pair and to search for clues as to who might have committed the double-murder. The safety of the village was interconnected to the safety of all who made the forest their home. The village owned the forest and was responsible for its safekeeping. If there was anything that men like Vilie could not take care of, it became the responsibility of the village council. In this spirit, they set off to do their duty of protecting and preventing further harm, if it was in their power.

Vilie was relieved he did not have to return with them. He had been very fond of the couple, and to be spared the additional trauma of burying their decaying bodies was something he was deeply grateful for.

At the insistence of the aunts, Vilie and Ate spent the

night in the village. Sitting in his aunts' kitchen and seeing
their grey-haired forms moving about, filled him with a
quiet joy. They were so happy to see him despite the sad
events that had forced him to return. He promised himself
and them that he would come more often. Though Selono
was the older of the two, Peleno looked more frail. Vilie
realised that they would not be around very much longer.

"Anyie," he said addressing Selono, "How old are you?
Do you have any idea?"

Selono stopped what she was doing and thought for a
while. She looked at her sister and back at Vilie, completely
at a loss for words.

"How would I know how old I am? The young pastor
was the first man to ask me that. I have no idea how old I
am. But your mother was not the same age-group as us.
She was in the age-group below ours. So how old does that
make me?"

Vilie reckoned she was around eighty-four and her
sister was probably eighty-two. They were the second
oldest people in the village, Selono added. It saddened
Vilie somewhat that he had let so many years slip by
before coming to see them. But the past years had been so
full of activity for him. There had been groups of hunters
regularly coming by when the rainy months eased off. In
fact even in the middle of the rains, some hunters had
come to try their luck. So he had been pretty occupied the
whole year round. Then the tragopan had kept him busy
because they were being hunted by men from another

village. Vilie had to be on vigil for many months, trying to track the culprits and provide their whereabouts to the Forest Department.

With the *gwi* he had not had many problems. It was part of his job to keep track of pregnant female-*gwi* and inform their owners when their cows birthed. There had only been one incident of a pack of wild dogs attacking *gwi* in these areas. He told them about the wild dog packs that roamed the Jotsoma forests and preyed on *gwi* calves. In the western areas, the villagers would go out in big groups and chase off the wild dog packs. Like every good *gwi* herder, Vilie stored salt and occasionally fed salt to the *gwi*.

There had been few cases of hunters shooting *gwi* by night mistaking them for other wildlife. In the past three years, that had happened twice, and both times Vilie had to find out who the owner was and negotiate compensation between the hunter and the owner. Since *gwi* were expensive animals, most hunters tried their best to avoid shooting them – though accidents did happen. Apart from the hunting season, Vilie was kept busy by hunters who came during the off-season to fish or try illegal hunting. He never approved of it and tried as much as he could to catch off-season hunters before they went too far.

When he finished recounting all he had been doing in the past years, it didn't sound like he had done very much. But they were all amazed that so much time had elapsed since they last saw each other. While they sat around the fire, Vilie reached into his bag and took out the heart-stone and showed it to the others. The stone glowed in the light of the fire and looked very beautiful.

"What is that?" asked both Peleno and Selono.

"This is a heart-stone. I plucked it from the riverbed on my last journey. I have been to the sleeping river. Have you heard of it?"

"The sleeping river? Of course we have," burst out Peleno. "There were some men from here who went looking for it. One of our cousins was in that group."

Vilie's face immediately lit up.

"Did he get it? Did he get the heart-stone?" he asked eagerly.

"Yes he actually did, but he lost it after some years, because some people were jealous of the great wealth of our cousin who owned most of the cattle in the village. The stone was probably stolen and taken to another village. We never saw it again after it went missing."

"What about your cousin? Did he lose his wealth?"

"No he did not lose his cattle, but his son was careless and did not look after them well. Eventually he sold off all the cattle and spent all the money on drink. He still lives in his father's old house, but it is run down and no longer as grand as it used to be."

Vilie held the stone up to the light again. It glinted in red, gold and purple lines. The red was a dark red, a rich, deep shade of red. He passed it to Ate. She looked at him while he opened the palm of her hand and laid it there.

"It's yours," Vilie said to her.

"No no, you mustn't give it away. Not after all you have gone through to get it!" she exclaimed.

She was so moved by his gesture that her voice was trembling as she spoke.

"It is that struggle that makes it all the more precious. I want you to have it. The heart-stone is in my heart. I have its knowledge carved into my heart, and no one can steal it from there."

She looked at him and mouthed thank you. Her voice had caught in her throat and her eyes glistened with unshed tears. She understood he was gifting her life, and the protection she would need to make it work well.

"Would you like to make this village your home?" Vilie suddenly asked Ate.

She was surprised at the question, and did not answer immediately. Peleno had heard the question and spoke up,

"Wasn't that the reason you came here? Of course she is very welcome to stay with us, or at your mother's house if she wants to live there – her and her baby."

Ate looked around at the two old women. They had simply taken her in without asking any questions. Her heart warmed toward them. If Vilie meant that she could not share his forest home with him, what better home would she find if she left this one? She could see that the two aunts were good human beings, happy to open up their home and share whatever food they had with them. She would do her share in caring for them, and bringing up the baby. They had not discussed finding another home for the baby, and she had never given that a thought. She had every intention of looking after him and giving him a home.

"We would never force anything on you, Ate. It was a thought that occurred to me very naturally because you seemed so at home here."

Vilie's voice drew her out of her thoughts. "You can also try living in my old house, and I will make sure the two of you are well provided for. The Forest Department pays me well enough."

"And you, Vilie? Would you come back here or would you continue to live on in the forest?" she wanted to know.

"You know I could lie and say I would come back too, just to make you stay. But you deserve honesty. I will not come back to live here. I am too used to the freedom that my forest life offers. But of course I would visit you frequently, and make sure you want for nothing."

Vilie had explained to the aunts that Ate had been taken away by Kirhupfümia when they were leaving her village, and he had brought her with him. That was the story the village would be told. The aunts were more than willing to take her in with the baby.

"You don't have to make a decision today, but it is something that is going to come up sooner or later so I thought I might as well ask you now."

But Ate had made up her mind. She would make the

village her home, and the old women she would embrace as family.

"I have no wish to find another home. I could not find any place more welcoming than this." Her eyes glistened with unshed tears as she said it, and her eyes fixed on Vilie betrayed no uncertainty.

"I know you will be happy here. I am sure of it," Vilie assured her.

The two sisters left no one in doubt that they were very happy with the arrangement. Their faces beamed as they passed the baby to each other, and though they tried not to show it, they had been keenly eavesdropping on the conversation between the younger people.

"They will have their own room. It's the room you always use when you come to visit. That is still empty, and the bed is made of good wood. It will last a lifetime." Selono was already making arrangements for Ate's stay.

"Thank you so much Anyie, you will not regret this. Your kindness will be repaid."

"From the Moment We are Born, We Begin to Die"

VILIE LEFT FOR THE FOREST the next morning in a peaceful frame of mind. He had not expected things to go so smoothly for Ate. But then Ate was different from girls of her age. She was very innocent about the world of humans, but mature in the things of the spirit. Vilie was certain she would be able to cope with village life, and she had the wisdom she needed to get around all the intricacies that community living demanded. He need not worry about her. Peleno and Selono would look after her well, and Ate and the boy would give the two aunts enough reason to live a little longer. Vibou was a tough little boy. He had proved that by surviving two days and nights without food and care. Vilie was confident he would make the village his world. He could go to school when he was big enough. Vilie remembered Krishna had said that he would not be sending his son to school, because he didn't have the money. Vilie intended to set that right. The two of them would be provided for. He had worked long enough for the Forest Department to earn a handsome pension, and it would go to supporting the two who had become family to him now.

Vilie took another route to his house not wanting to go back to the Nepali settlement. It was a shorter route than the one that went through the woodcutter's house. But Vilie had always used the other one, because it rewarded him with the company of his two friends. Now there was no reason not to take the shorter route.

The vegetation was less dense in this part of the forest. The big trees had been cut down to be sawn into planks. He had a better view through the partially deforested areas. Vilie was a tracker. He easily picked up clues like unusual footprints and recently discarded cigarette butts. The killing was on his mind and he stayed alert to signs that would reveal that a stranger had been in these woods. But he found no such signs. One conclusion was that the killer might have left the area, and was possibly quite far away now. The council members who had gone to investigate the murder, said that the couple had most likely been robbed of money because there was no money found in the house. The woman was missing the gold necklace that married Nepali women always wore. Gone too were her gold earrings, and that gave the council the conclusion that the double murder was motivated by robbery.

There had been talk that the village planned to cultivate the areas that were being deforested. This would become a reality in the wake of the killings, because that was a way of providing security to the forest dwellers. If they had more neighbours and more people working in the vicinity, they would not be so isolated and so vulnerable to attacks. It was the isolation that partly encouraged this sort of crime. Many discussions had taken place in the village council in relation to the safety of the forest dwellers, and the village's responsibility to look after them. However, Vilie did not feel threatened by the killings. He did not have much, at least not enough to tempt anyone to try and murder him, and make off with his belongings. He had never been robbed before. Anyway, why was he thinking about this so much? He rebuked himself and quickened his pace.

There was the house ahead of him. It was early evening when he reached, and it pleased him to have made such good time. He went into the house and lay his bag down. There was enough time to check his traps before the light went, so he walked over to see if any small animal had been caught. A big mongoose was lying in the pit, but it looked like it had been dead for some days. Vilie decided to bury it instead. For now he had enough dry meat to last him for some time. He fetched his spade from the house, dug a deep hole, pulled the mongoose out and buried it. He then returned to the house to prepare a meal. Everything was still at this dusk hour. The birds had finished roosting, and the night insects were yet to begin their cheeping. Vilie sat on the steps waiting for the water to boil.

The crackle of dry leaves crushed under a boot betrayed

the presence of another person. Vilie's hearing had become particularly sharp after he had battled the multitude of spirits in the bid to save Ate. Vilie stood up and walked towards the sound. There was a man standing with a bag slung on his shoulder.

"Are you the forest guard?" he asked in an unpleasant tone of voice. It was not a polite query. Vilie fought back resentment as he made reply.

"That's me. Do you have any business here?"

The man stepped out of the darkness and stood looking at Vilie. He had a belligerent look about him. Vilie wondered if he should invite him in or not. Under normal circumstances he would have invited the stranger in, and shared his food with him. But now he hesitated. There was something about the stranger that he didn't trust at all, and the hair on his neck rose up when the man spoke. He was not tall, not as tall as Vilie but he was very well built. The muscles stood out on him as he walked out of the shadow of the trees, and into the dying light of the evening.

"I want to make a deal with you," he began and reached into his bag.

"Here is money. I know you have the heart-stone. The Nepali couple told me about that. I will buy it from you." He raised a bundle of notes and showed it to Vilie.

"I don't intend to trade with it," Vilie answered carefully and straightened his shoulders.

His mind was racing. If he said it was not with him, the man would suspect it was with Ate, and she would be in danger. He had no doubt that this was the killer. The man had a deadly cold look in his eyes. Vilie feared he would stop at nothing to get the heart-stone, even killing again.

"You know who I am, don't you? I killed them both, husband and wife. They said you had gone to get the stone and were on your way back."

"The heart-stone is not for the likes of you," Vilie said angrily. "It is not for working evil. It is to be used to spread goodness."

"Oh really? That is not what I heard," sneered the intruder as he came menacingly closer.

Vilie debated whether he had time to run for his gun, or if he should use his spade to defend himself.

"That's right, get your gun and threaten me with it," snarled the man as though reading his thoughts. "You're not much of a man without your gun, are you?"

He came closer until he was a few feet away. Vilie began to back towards the house. He was getting the gun no matter what the man thought.

They both sprang in the same instant, Vilie for his gun, and the stranger, knife raised to strike him. In the next instant, he was on top of Vilie pinning him down as Vilie struggled desperately to free himself. Vilie felt a sharp stab in his side and the searing pain that followed arrested his struggle. The man had a long knife with which he stabbed Vilie again and again, with the ease of a man skilled at using the deadly weapon. The brutal assault suddenly ended when the intruder was knocked to the ground by a tremendous blow.

The killer had been so preoccupied with Vilie that he never saw the tiger until it was too late. Leaping out of the forest, the weretiger pounced on its prey and iron claws ripped into helpless skin. The white avenger was relentless as it clawed the life out of the terrified man so that all that was left of him were the clothes on his back, and some tendons vainly hanging onto exposed bone.

FIFTY

Burying the Undead

WHEN VILIE DID NOT RETURN to the village for the third day, his worried clansmen set out for his forest dwelling. They found what they suspected was his dead body mauled beyond recognition, and fast decomposing.

"This is terrible!" Kelethuzo exclaimed. "The killer must have been waiting for him!"

"Vilie did not deserve this," Vibi, the other clansman echoed. "What shall we do?"

"We have to bury him here. We can't let his aunts and the girl see him like this." Kelethuzo said in a decided manner.

The other men quickly agreed with him. In any case there was nothing resembling a human being left of the dead man. They all realised this was one instance when they could not fulfil the Tenyimia ritual of taking their dead home to the village to be buried in the ancestral courtyard. But they would take with them some of his belongings, and a bit of his hair and perform the funeral rites in the village.

"Looks like the jackals got at him after the killing," Vibi remarked. Bits of human flesh and bone lay on the ground near the mutilated body.

"We had best bury everything quickly before the animals return looking for more."

The burial was not a long affair. The men were not conducting a funeral. They were carrying out the practical task of burying human remains, so that tigers or bears would not be able to feed on it and get a taste of human flesh. When that was done, they went into the house and checked for signs of burglary but nothing looked disturbed. Vilie was a tidy householder. Things seemed to be in its place, although dust had settled on the furniture to indicate the house had not been lived in for a long time. The two guns, however, were gone.

"What did the killer want?" Vibi asked as they went through the house.

"Difficult to say," Kelethuzo replied, "Vilie had his guns and a good stash of ammunition. Not much money though. Hard to guess what the killer was hoping to get by killing a fine man like Vilie. This must be the same man who killed the Nepali couple and made off with their possessions. Quite obviously he has taken the guns with him."

They slowly walked to the corner of the room where Vilie's bed was. Vibi kicked at a large stain on the floor.

"What's that?" Kelethuzo asked curiously as he bent down to take a closer look.

"Looks like blood!" he exclaimed. It was a blackened mass of dried blood.

"It is blood!" Vibi cried out.

"If he was killed out there, why is there blood in the house? This is very strange." Kelethuzo said to the others.

"Could he have injured himself before he was attacked?"

After this discovery they found that the dark brown stains led all the way from the steps to the house.

Apart from the blood mass there were no signs of a struggle, no clues on the wood floor or the rest of the room. Where had the blood come from? Holding up his gun, Kelethuzo walked to the shelves on the wall. He pulled off the curtain that covered the shelves. Nothing there. Nothing under the bed either. The two men walked back to their waiting friend.

Their immediate task was to take the news back to the village, and break it to his kith and kin. It was not their job to try and solve the murder. In any case, the killer could be miles away from here by now. It was now the responsibility of the village council, as the matter of making the forest safe for the forest dwellers was a council affair.

They collected some of Vilie's things, a body cloth and his bag that they found on the porch with its contents intact. Having collected all that, they locked the door to the first room, and began their long walk back to the village.

The sun was going down by the time they reached the first roadside shed.

When they reached the village it was very late. The fires in the houses had almost all gone out, so they postponed their unpleasant task of informing the family. Tomorrow they would mourn the hunter guardian in the manner he deserved to be mourned.

The Heart of the Stone

THREE PEOPLE WALKED INTO THE CLEARING where the forest house stood. They stood there silently for some minutes. Suddenly the boy ran to the porch and began to play with a pile of wood shavings in the corner.

"Careful you don't prick your finger on a nail, Vibou!" his mother called out.

The house looked unused and abandoned. The back of the house was coming apart. The thatch roof had fallen away and the bamboo structure was broken in places. The only room that still looked sturdy was the one in front, which had been the extra room for guests. It had a tin roof which had withstood the elements.

"So you come here once in every four or five months?" the young man asked the woman by his side. She looked a little older than the girl who had been left by the forest guardian in the village five years ago. The swell of her stomach showed that she was at least six or seven months pregnant.

"Yes. Every quarter of a year for four years now."

"Have you ever seen your father again?"

"No, but I know he didn't die in the fight."

"Really? How do you know the body they found was not his? How are you so sure?"

The woman did not reply immediately. She looked over at the house and her gaze turned to the woods beyond. There was a dreamy look in her eyes as she turned back to the man.

"I don't know, I can't explain it. I just know."

"Amazing," the young man said shaking his head. His name was Asakho. He had been married to Ate for a little over half a year now.

"Ate, sometimes you refer to him as your father and other times you call him by name. Why is that?"

"Well, he was not my biological father, but he was the greatest life-giving source I ever knew. So he was a father to me in that sense. He was also the kindest man I knew."

"Who else besides you suspects the forest guardian might still be alive?"

"Remember the young hunter Roko? He was here some weeks ago. He said he felt a presence in the house which was not frightening but different. He actually referred to it as companionable. Imagine that."

"Well it could have been anything. Perhaps it was an especially warm evening?"

"I very much doubt that. It was midwinter then. Besides, I trust that Roko would tell me the truth."

"What about the heart-stone? Did Vilie worship it? What was the mystery of the stone?"

"The stone is not an object of worship. That is the mistake many people make with it. It is not for making profit for oneself. Before his journey, Vilie kept dreaming repeatedly that he was at the sleeping river plucking the stone from the river water. He felt sure he was destined to get the stone, and that was why he went on the journey, and he did find the river and the heart-stone. The wisdom of the stone is more spiritual than physical. It helps us discover the spiritual identity that is within us, so we can use it to combat the dark forces that are always trying to control and suppress us. But men who are not initiated don't understand this about the stone, and they try to use it to gain wealth and other material things. Vilie was already using the stone on our journey back here. I mean he was using the knowledge he had gotten from his adventure with the stone."

Their talk was interrupted by the boy trying to clamber up the wooden railing. Vibou was tired of playing with the wood shavings and was attempting to climb into the guest room. His mother shouted anxiously,

"Vibou! That's dangerous! Wait, I'll help you!" Ate ran to Vibou and lifted him over the wood railing of the guest room. She then crossed over the railing herself and they found themselves standing inside the guest room. There was a bed and a table, but not much else. Ate had earlier removed and burnt piles of old bedclothes, because she did not want some careless hunter to start a fire that would burn the house down. The bed was there for anyone to use if they needed to. There was a rough jute mat on top of it. In the kitchen, none of the utensils had been removed. From time to time, a group of hunters would come by and use the house, but they made sure to tidy it before they left, showing their respect to the former owner of the house.

Asakho stepped into the room.

"I could fix up the place if you want. It won't need more than a week's work."

"Oh would you do that? I know he would want nothing more than for this house to provide shelter and comfort to travellers that come to this area," Ate said.

"It's settled then, I will fix up the shelves in the kitchen and the walls and roof. Neipekreizo can help me and the work will go quickly."

"Thank you. Vilie would be very pleased. I really don't want this house to fall apart."

He looked at her and saw tears in her eyes.

"He was so important to you, wasn't he?"

"Oh yes, he opened up my mind to the possibility of a whole new existence. I mean apart from saving my life twice! We have gone through the valley of the shadow of death together – in a manner of speaking."

"I'll always regret never having met him."

Their attention was diverted by Vibou climbing on the bed, and attempting to climb the table by standing on the headboard. Ate went over to him and lifted him onto the table.

"What will you do up there, my little man?"

Predictably, he was soon bored and asked to be helped down to the floor. This she did and he ran off to play with a toy car, pushing it along the floor to the outer door and back again. He would be preoccupied for some time with the repetitive movement.

"Ate," Asakho began again in a low voice, "when did you leave the heart-stone here? How do you know he has gotten it and not someone else?" he asked reopening their disrupted conversation.

"I brought it back on my second visit and hid it in the main room. The same night I had a dream and I knew I had done the right thing. It was no longer there when I returned the next time."

"Did anyone suspect you might have it?"

"Only a few people knew that I had the heart-stone with me. Anyie Selono and Anyie Peleno have seen it, but I doubt they will remember that Vilie gave it to me in their kitchen. They are both so old now and their memories are not what they used to be. Roko has seen it once. He admired Vilie very much. At his funeral, he was heart-broken and vowed to find the killer. Apart from those three, no one else has seen it in my possession."

"Have you told Roko what you did with it?"

"No, not yet. Vilie was very good to him and there is no reason for him to try and harm me."

"I think you should let him know," Asakho looked serious.

"I will do that as soon as we get back." she promised.

"Do you think Vibou might want to go looking for the heart-stone when he grows up?"

They looked at him and looked at each other and smiled. At the moment he was so boisterous it was hard to imagine him as a grown up, making wise decisions for himself and others.

"He just might become a very good hunter," Ate spoke thoughtfully, "He has a fierce enough heart and you would teach him to be patient."

"That will take some teaching," Asakho declared looking at the boy. But Ate knew he had come to love Vibou as his own and the little boy always called him Apuo, father.

"But he will need a companion for such a journey and I wouldn't allow him to travel without his brother," she said, placing a hand over her stomach.

Her husband's eyes widened in surprise.

"You're sure it is going to be a boy?"

"Well, the stone will need a hunter to protect it from evil men. What could be better than two protectors instead of just the one?"

Glossary of Words in Tenyidie

Ketsaga	from the same species as Tree fern, *Dicksonia antartica*
Gwi	the mithun is also called Indian bison, *Bos frontalis*, found in the Naga Hills,
Tierhutiepfü	Amaranth, *Amaranthus viridis*, a curative herb,
Tekhumiavi	weretiger, a phenomenon amongst the Tenyimia people where certain members of the tribe transform their spirits into tigers.
Age-group house	the educational institution of the village whereby children of the same age are taught by an elder, known as a parent. The house is an actual house where they are encouraged to spend the night, listening to stories and learning the ways of the tribe.
Kesüni	black men's kilt, decorated with white cowries in rows
Vilhuü nha	Redflower ragleaf or Fireweed, *Crassocephalum crepidioides*

Japan nha	Crofton weed, *Eupatorium adenophorum*. Good for malaria, stomach ache, hæmostatic. The leaf paste is applied on cuts and wounds. Japan nha is also microbicidial.
Tsomhou	Nutgall tree, *Rhus chinensis*, medicinal shrub.
Ciena	Bitter wormwood.
Rock bee honey	*Apis dorsata*, speeds up healing, speeds growth of healing tissue and dries up wounds.
Tathu	a savoury side dish made of roasted ingredients like chilli, fish, tomato, native spring onions etc.
Jotho	*Elatostema,* edible species of the nettle family
Rarhuria	literally means unclean place, name given to certain forest areas
Gara	Indian pennywort, *Centella asiatica*
Gapa	Great plantain, *Plantago erosa*
Genna day	a day declared as a no-work day. It is a taboo to work on genna days and the cultural belief is that those who violate genna days are punished with injuries and accidents that have even resulted in death
Dao	Long handled machete used by the Nagas
Ukepenuopfü/ Kepenuopfü	The birth-spirit, the supreme God worshipped by the Tenyimia in the old religion. The same name is used for the Christian God.

Terhuomia pezie	Thanks to the spirits, pronounced like a prayer of thanksgiving, like a grace to acknowledge the giver of food from the forest or farms.
Kepenuopfii zanu tsie la mhatalie	In the name of the creator, retreat at once.
Senyiega	Tree fern, *Dicksonia antartica*
Tenyimia	largest linguistic group of nine tribes sharing the same language, Tenyidie.
Mezasi	June plum, Tahitian apple and Polynesian are its several names. *Spondias dulcis*
Anie	paternal uncle. Tenyimia never address older people by their names.
Kirhupfümia	A minority group of women thought to have the power of maiming, blinding or killing people simply by pointing at them with their fingers.
Vizonhie	standard greeting meaning, Are you well?
Anyie	paternal aunt
Hou	expression used to express a range of emotions from sympathy to surprise or shock and outrage.
Native Tobacco	*Nicotiana tabacum*, used as insecticide, sedative, antinflammatory, anthelminitic, carminative, laxative, mental stimulants and relieves rheumatic swelling.